# WHERE INK HESITATES

Kankona Chakraborty

**BLUEROSE PUBLISHERS**
India | U.K.

Copyright © Kankona Chakraborty 2025

All rights reserved by author. No part of this publication may be reproduced, stored in a retrieval system or transmitted in any form or by any means, electronic, mechanical, photocopying, recording or otherwise, without the prior permission of the author. Although every precaution has been taken to verify the accuracy of the information contained herein, the publisher assumes no responsibility for any errors or omissions. No liability is assumed for damages that may result from the use of information contained within.

BlueRose Publishers takes no responsibility for any damages, losses, or liabilities that may arise from the use or misuse of the information, products, or services provided in this publication.

For permissions requests or inquiries regarding this publication, please contact:

BLUEROSE PUBLISHERS
www.BlueRoseONE.com
info@bluerosepublishers.com
+91 8882 898 898
+4407342408967

ISBN: 978-93-6783-866-2

First Edition: January 2025

# Acknowledgment

Thank you to my grandmother for her wisdom, my father for his unwavering support, and my friend Cham for being an exceptional proof-reader. Your love, belief, and effort have made this book possible.

*"Between the lines, where stories live and*

*souls meet, I found you."*

*I wish I were a poem,*
*A poem with love in its heart;*
*And beauty in spaces between its words.*
*I wish I had the beauty,*
*That a poet sees in a withering flower;*
*And not in a blossoming bud.*
*I wish to be the ink on his paper;*
*Dark, but writes eternal words.*

*If my pretty face wasn't my personality,*
*If my silken hair wasn't my identity,*
*And if 'beauty' didn't define me;*
*Maybe I would've been beautiful.*
*Beauty, I wish I could lose it*
*And be known for the way my heart weeps.*

# Playlist

# Contents

1. Alasdair ........................................................................ 1
2. Alasdair ...................................................................... 10
3. Alasdair ...................................................................... 16
4. Alasdair ...................................................................... 21
5. Seraphine ................................................................... 27
6. Seraphine ................................................................... 36
7. Seraphine ................................................................... 41
8. Seraphine ................................................................... 45
9. Alasdair ...................................................................... 49
10. Seraphine ................................................................. 56
11. Alasdair .................................................................... 63
12. Seraphine ................................................................. 67
13. Alasdair .................................................................... 73
14. Seraphine ................................................................. 80
15. Alasdair .................................................................... 84
16. Alasdair .................................................................... 90
17. Alasdair .................................................................... 95
18. Alasdair .................................................................. 101
19. Alasdair .................................................................. 105
20. Alasdair .................................................................. 113
21. Alasdair .................................................................. 121
22. Alasdair .................................................................. 130
23. Alasdair .................................................................. 137
24. Alasdair .................................................................. 143
25. Alasdair .................................................................. 149

26. Alasdair ................................................................. 153
27. Alasdair ................................................................. 159
28. Alasdair ................................................................. 164
29. Alasdair ................................................................. 172
30. Alasdair ................................................................. 177
31. Alasdair ................................................................. 184
32. Alasdair ................................................................. 194
33. Seraphine ............................................................... 199
34. Seraphine ............................................................... 205
35. Seraphine ............................................................... 207
36. Seraphine ............................................................... 212
37. Seraphine ............................................................... 217
38. Seraphine ............................................................... 224

# 1
## Alasdair

My life felt like a looped song over the past days. I felt like the loop option on Spotify would exhaust itself, but my life wouldn't. Day after day, I sat there, fiddling with my pen, staring at a blank page, hoping for something—anything—to come. The words seemed stuck somewhere deep inside, tangled and unreachable. Every once in a while, a sentence stumbled out, but it never felt good enough to keep.

And then came the mountain that followed—the part where someone else had to believe in the thing I poured myself into. Publishers, agents, reviewers—they didn't even look twice. My inbox was filled with polite rejections, or worse, silence. It was as if my voice had no place in the world of noise, as if I was writing into a void that refused to write back.

The block, though—that was the hardest part. It was not just about not knowing what to write. It was the weight of everything: the self-doubt, the deadlines, the fear that maybe I'd already written the best thing I'd ever write. The pen felt heavier in my hand, and the paper stared back like it knew.

Sometimes I wondered if I'd ever break through it, or if that was just what being a writer truly was—fighting to believe in yourself when no one else did.

My thoughts put a heavy strain on my mind. The day felt like any other—grey, unremarkable, and filled with a familiar sense of dread that had become routine. I stared at the ceiling, letting the minutes blur together. The world outside was moving, but I wasn't. My phone buzzed on the table, snapping me out of my haze and pulling me reluctantly back into the moment.

"Happy birthday, dude!" Albert's voice blasted through the speaker, cheerful, loud, and entirely out of sync with my mood.

"What?" I mumbled, still half-dazed, sitting up slowly. "It's my birthday?"

"Yeah, man. December 17th. Ring a bell?"

I blinked, glancing at the calendar on my desk. Sure enough, there it was, circled in bright red—a detail my own mind had somehow chosen to ignore. It didn't feel like a day worth celebrating.

"Huh," I said flatly, rubbing my face as if trying to wake myself up. "Guess it is."

"Wow. Way to be excited. Come on, it's your day! Let's do something crazy!"

Crazy. Right. My gaze fell on the piles of papers and unfinished drafts cluttering my desk. I barely had the energy to sit upright, let alone embrace the idea of celebrations.

"So, what do you want me to do? Dance?" I muttered, pinching the bridge of my nose. "I'm drowning in stress, dude."

"Relax," Albert chuckled. "I've sent you something. A cake and a little gift. Should be there soon. Just try to enjoy it, alright?"

Before I could respond, the line went dead. Typical Albert. Always signing off on his own terms, leaving no room for arguments.

I stared at my phone for a long moment, still holding it as if expecting him to call back. My birthday? It was just another reminder of how little had changed. I felt older but not wiser, more tired but no closer to the life I wanted.

The doorbell rang, pulling me from my spiral. I shuffled to the door, my body moving on autopilot. A parcel sat on the doorstep, neatly wrapped with a handwritten note taped to the top.

"Open this, eat the cake, and remember you're not alone. Happy birthday, you grump. – Albert."

I let out a small, reluctant laugh as I brought the parcel inside. Trust Albert to be the only bright spot on a day like this.

Curiosity tugged at me as I tore open the wrapping. Inside, there was a cake, simple and homemade-looking, and a book. The title gleamed in elegant gold letters: To Be a Poem.

I ran my fingers over the cover, flipping through the pages almost instinctively. The faint scent of fresh ink rose as I skimmed over a few lines. It didn't take long to realise that it was related to romance. I sighed, shaking my head, and picked up my phone.

"Seriously? Romance?" I said as soon as Albert picked up.

"Just read it, will you? It's a bestseller!" he shot back, his tone exasperated but amused.

"I don't even read romance," I grumbled. "I'm not running from it—I just haven't found it yet. And honestly? I'm starting to doubt if I ever will. Maybe my so-called 'soulmate' doesn't even exist."

"Wow," Albert said, dragging out the word like he was trying to process my entire life's disappointment. "That's a depressing take. Stop being a fool for once and just appreciate the damn gift. Read the book, okay? Who knows, it might surprise you."

"Alright, alright," I relented, slumping back into my chair. "But if I hate it, I'm blaming you."

"Deal," he laughed. "But you won't."

As I hung up, the book sat there on the table, waiting. Its cover stared back at me like a dare, as if it knew something I didn't. A part of me wanted to ignore it, to brush it off like every other attempt at celebrating my birthday. But for the first time in a long while, I felt a flicker of curiosity.

Maybe Albert was right. Maybe, just maybe, this book was more than it seemed.

The day seemed to slip through my fingers as I tried to focus on completing my work. Every passing moment felt like a race against time, yet somehow, the hours stretched endlessly, creating a strange duality. The clock ticked on steadily, but my mind swung between a sense of urgency and an overwhelming stillness, as though caught in the tension of too much to do and too little time to feel grounded.

As the clock struck midnight and the world around me grew quiet, I finally decided to pick up the book that had been waiting patiently on my desk. The soft glow of the lamp cast warm shadows across the pages, and for a moment, the weight of the day melted away. The stillness of the night seemed to invite me into the world of the story, offering an escape from the lingering thoughts that had occupied my mind throughout the day. With a deep breath, I opened the book, ready to lose myself in its words. I hadn't placed much expectation on the book when I started, assuming it would be little more than a fleeting distraction. Yet, there was something about it—an unexplainable pull that gripped me. It wasn't loud or obvious, but it lingered, like a soft current beneath still waters, urging me to keep turning the pages.

*I'm getting married.* That was the first line. "What a weird way to start a book," I murmured.

*I love him. Loved him for years. I look at him with hearty eyes. When I stare at his face, my heart feels warm like a comforting cup of coffee in mid-December. But when he looks at me, somehow, his eyes don't feel like they're on me. As if he's looking into my eyes, but his mind is somewhere else. He stares so deeply that anyone would believe that he's in love with me. But when I meet his gaze, something is missing. The warmth, the glimmer, the look of love.*

It left me feeling hollow, a strange mix of sadness and frustration. Here I was, with my heart aching, yearning for a love I could never quite reach, while somewhere out there, someone was basking in the warmth of that very love, only to take it for granted. It felt cruel, almost unjust—how one heart could overflow with love, only to be ignored, while another silently mourned in its absence.

Before I knew it, I was completely lost in the book. The story gripped me in ways I hadn't anticipated, pulling me deeper with every turn of the page. The quiet hum of the night faded into the background, and the world around me seemed to dissolve, leaving only the vivid images painted by the words on the page. I barely noticed the hours slipping by—time had become irrelevant. It wasn't until the sharp, jarring sound of my morning alarm pierced through my trance that I realised how deeply I had been immersed. Blinking against the sudden light creeping through the curtains, I glanced at the clock, astonished to see that the entire night had vanished without me noticing.

I softly closed the book and kept it on my nightstand. Getting up from the bed, I went to the bathroom and freshened myself up. I dressed quickly, pulling on my best shirt, the one I'd ironed with care the night before. It was nothing fancy, but it was clean and pressed. I grabbed my manuscript, fingers lingering on the edges of the pages like it was something fragile, something that could be torn apart by the harshness of the world. But I couldn't let myself dwell on that now. Today was the day. I had to believe that.

The train ride was long and monotonous, giving me far too much time to think. I went over my pitch in my head again and again, each time trying to smooth out the edges and make it sound just right. But the words started to feel like stones in my mouth—too heavy, too unpolished. No matter how many times I told myself it would be okay, I knew deep down that nothing was ever truly certain.

When I finally reached the publishing house, the building towered over me, sleek and cold, as if daring me to step inside. The receptionist barely acknowledged my presence as she gave me directions to the waiting area. I sank into the uncomfortable chair, trying to steady my breathing. My heart raced in my chest, thumping in a rhythm I couldn't control.

Minutes passed, maybe hours, before a man in a suit appeared. He barely looked at me as he extended a hand, his face impassive, unreadable.

"Let's get this over with," he said, already pulling my manuscript from my bag before I even had a chance to settle in.

The meeting was brief—too brief. He barely skimmed the pages, flicking through them as though they held no more weight than a leaflet. And then, without missing a beat, he looked up at me and said, "It's not what we're looking for."

His voice was final. Detached.

I wanted to say something, to defend my work, to explain how much it meant to me. But the words didn't come. It felt as though I was speaking into a void, the editor's eyes distant and uninterested. I tried to push on, to find a way to convince him, but it was pointless.

The meeting ended quickly, just as coldly as it had started. I left the office feeling like a failure, clutching my manuscript like it was the only thing holding me together. The city outside felt like a blur, too loud, too fast. I wasn't sure where I was heading, but I knew I wasn't going to stop. Not yet. Maybe the next door would open, or maybe the one after that. But I'd keep trying. I had no choice.

By the time I finally reached home, the day had slipped into the evening. The light outside had softened into a dusky glow. The sky, once bright and full of possibility, had turned a muted shade of purple, signalling that time had moved on without me even realising it. I stood outside my apartment for a moment, staring at the worn building in front of me. The weight of the rejection still pressed down on my chest, but there was a certain numbness that had settled in, too.

I hadn't even noticed how fast the hours had passed as I walked through the city, lost in my thoughts.

When I opened the door to my apartment, the silence that greeted me felt heavier than usual. The smell of stale coffee lingered in the air, a reminder of mornings spent hoping that today would be different. I dropped my bag by the door, the manuscript still inside, untouched and unused. The room felt emptier than I remembered, as if it, too, could sense my defeat.

I sank onto the couch, letting out a breath I didn't realise I'd been holding. The dim light from the window barely illuminated the room, and I let my eyes wander over the clutter—old papers, half-finished projects, scattered thoughts that I hadn't cleaned up in weeks. It was the kind of space where dreams could be put away, forgotten, only to resurface when the silence got too loud.

I made my way to my bedroom, the exhaustion from the day creeping in with every step. I hadn't slept the night before, my mind too restless, too tangled in thoughts of the meeting, the rejection, and the uncertainty of what came next. The bed, unmade and inviting, seemed like the only place where I could finally escape the weight of it all. I barely had the energy to change into anything comfortable—just slipping under the covers in the clothes I had worn all day.

I reached for my phone and put on some soft, calming music. The familiar sound of gentle piano notes filled the room. The music, though soothing, couldn't entirely chase away the thoughts still buzzing in my head. But it did help, dulling the sharp edges of my frustration and disappointment just enough to give me some space to breathe.

I closed my eyes, the rhythm of the music matching the slow, steady beat of my heart. The tension in my body slowly began to melt away, but the sadness stayed, like a low hum in the background. I felt my body sink into the mattress, the exhaustion finally catching up to me. My limbs grew heavy, and my eyelids fluttered shut. I couldn't remember the last time I had felt this drained, physically and emotionally.

Sleep, when it came, was quiet and unremarkable. There were no vivid dreams, no restless tossing and turning—just a deep, overwhelming stillness that I needed more than anything. As the world outside faded into darkness, I let go of everything for just a few hours, slipping into the kind of sleep that only comes when you've reached the end of your rope.

## 2
## Alasdair

When I woke up the next morning, the soft light filtering through the curtains seemed almost like an invitation to start over. I slowly opened my eyes, letting them adjust to the room. My gaze naturally drifted to my nightstand, where the book I'd been reading sat. Its cover, now familiar, looked almost like an old friend waiting for me to return. I smiled to myself, feeling a sense of comfort wash over me. Something about it, the way it had captured me, taken me away from the weight of the world for just a while felt like a small refuge.

I let out a sigh and stretched, shaking off the remnants of a restless sleep. The day ahead was uncertain, filled with the same questions and doubts as yesterday, but at that moment, the book was a small piece of peace. I swung my legs over the side of the bed and stood up, the hardwood floor cool beneath my feet. Without thinking too much about it, I made my way to the kitchen.

I brewed myself a cup of coffee, the rich aroma filling the air as it bubbled and hissed in the pot. It was a small, simple ritual, but one I found grounding. The sound of the coffee dripping into the pot, the warm steam rising, was a comfort in itself. I poured the dark brew into my favourite mug, the one with the chipped edge that I'd had for years. As I took my first sip, the warmth spread through me, a much-needed remedy to the weariness from yesterday.

With the cup in hand, I returned to my bedroom, sitting down by the window where the sunlight was now spilling onto the floor. I picked up the book and opened it to the page I'd left off, letting the words draw me in again. There was something about the simplicity of the moment—just me, a cup of coffee, and a good book—that made everything feel a little more bearable. For a while, I could forget about the world outside and simply exist in this small, comforting space.

*Today, for the first time in a year he touched me. On my cheek. I felt his cold fingertips on my soft skin leaving a mark. Leaving fingerprints, red and almost visible. It stung a little but soon I felt honoured to at least feel the touch of the person I love.*

"Did he hit her?" I blurted out loud, my voice louder than I intended as my eyes widened in disbelief. I couldn't pull my gaze from the page, the words leaving a strange, unsettling sensation in my chest. Until now, I had thought this was just another romance novel, a familiar tale of love and longing. But as the plot twisted, it became clear that there was something deeper, something darker unfolding between the characters. The rawness of it all, the emotions swirling on the pages, felt so real, so visceral, that I couldn't shake the feeling it was more than just fiction.

As an author myself, I knew the struggle of writing something authentic—how every sentence carries a piece of you, even if you don't consciously realise it. It's impossible to write with such depth unless you've lived through something similar, or at least felt it. And in that moment, I couldn't help but wonder: was this the author's own pain, their own experiences hidden between the lines? Was this a reflection of something they had endured, perhaps a piece of their soul quietly laid bare in the story?

The depth of emotion in this book felt too personal. It was as though the author had poured their own heartache into the narrative, giving life to every conflict, every struggle, every fragile moment. I could almost sense their presence in the words, the way they had channeled their scars into the characters, turning pain into something beautiful—and heartbreaking—on the page. It made me wonder if the love they wrote about was a way of healing, a way of rewriting their own story, or maybe even confronting their own demons. Either way, it was impossible to ignore the sense that this story wasn't just fictional; it was a mirror to something real.

*Today is the happiest day of my life. I had been longing for his touch for a long time. Every brush of his skin against mine widened my smile. My mouth smiled but my eyes didn't. They shed tears. They were the tears of love... or were they?*

"Oh dear..." I sighed. "That's not love, that's pain," I said, as if she could hear me. My voice felt futile. I wanted it to reach her but I knew that it stayed only with myself.

The further I read, the more it felt less like a book and more like a cry for help. But what help could I provide to the unknown? The book didn't feel like fiction. It felt like a letter—a quiet confession only I was meant to read.

*I still remember the day we got engaged. I still laugh when I think of it. The ring was too small for me. Also, it was silver, even though I only wear gold. It felt as if the ring was made for someone else. Funny, right?*

*"Asher. You know that I only wear gold, right? Then mind if I ask why my ring is silver?" I asked him politely, with a small smile tugging on my face.*

*"For once, can you be appreciative? Is it not enough that I got you one? You're always asking for more." He said, his tone angry and annoyed.*

*"Oh... I'm sorry. I didn't mean to be disrespectful."*

*"Please get out of my sight for now. I loathe your presence."*

"Is he nuts?" I thought, my disbelief growing with every passing second. The way he treated her, as though her feelings were something insignificant, was beyond me. If I were him, there's no way I'd ever allow her to shed a tear, not for anything. I would've moved mountains to keep her smiling, to make sure she never felt that kind of hurt. But there he was, oblivious to the pain he was causing, indifferent to the fragile heart right in front of him. The unfairness of it all gnawed at me. How could someone who claimed to care let someone they loved suffer so easily?

*My whole life, I had been searching for love—the kind of love that makes everything else fade into the background. I had always dreamed of that feeling, the one where you know, deep down, that you are someone's entire world, their reason to smile, their inspiration. The kind of love where every touch, every word, feels like a verse of poetry, something beautifully crafted just for you. I wanted to be someone's poem—an intimate, eternal reflection of their feelings, a story told in the most delicate, powerful words.*

*I longed to feel like I belonged, not just to someone, but to their heart, in a way that felt sacred and unwavering. It wasn't just about finding affection—it was about finding that deep connection, where the world outside could crumble, and still, everything would feel right because you had each other. I wanted to be the one they couldn't stop thinking about, the one they could never express enough because no words would ever truly capture how much they felt for me.*

*But as I searched, it always felt elusive, like chasing shadows in the fading light. I'd had glimpses of it, moments when love seemed so close, but something always kept it out of reach. And now, standing at the edge of something that seemed like it could have been that perfect love, I realised that maybe I had been searching for the wrong kind of affection all along. I wanted to be more than just loved—I wanted to be cherished, understood, and valued in a way that no one could take away. And for that, I wasn't sure where to turn.*

The way her words flowed so naturally, the way her characters spoke of love and loss, of hope and regret—it was as if every sentence had been crafted with a tenderness only someone who had truly lived could understand. I could feel her in every line, the pain she had endured, the dreams she had longed for, and the love that had somehow eluded her. It was in the way she described every moment, each emotion as if she had lived it herself.

But it wasn't just the beauty of her writing that held me captivated—it was the realisation that somehow, in a way I couldn't fully explain, I was a part of this story. Her words, while deeply personal, seemed to reach out and speak to me, as if she had woven me into the fabric of her narrative without even knowing it. I wondered if she had written this for someone like me, or if I was simply interpreting it in my own way, searching for meaning in the spaces between the words.

As I turned another page, I felt a longing rise within me. I wanted to tell her how much her writing had affected me, how much it had opened my eyes to her, to the person she was beneath the surface. I wanted to show her that I understood her pain, her hope, and her desires, not just through the words in the book, but through my actions. I wanted to be the one who could give her the love that had been missing in her life, to show her that she didn't have to carry it all alone.

But for now, I was just here, reading her story, hoping that one day she would know how deeply I felt for her and how much I wished to be a part of her world.

## 3
## Alasdair

Love for me had been like fog—dense, elusive, almost invisible. It always hovered just beyond my reach, lingering in the background like a distant shadow, never fully forming, never fully tangible. The moments when it seemed clear, when it felt close, were fleeting, like glimpsing something through the mist—just enough to make me yearn for it more, but never enough to touch. The little visibility that had been there, those rare moments when I had seen its outline, was nothing but hope. Hope, fragile and persistent, like a flickering light in the distance, guiding me forward, promising that it existed even when it felt too far away to grasp.

I had spent so many years trying to navigate through that fog, following the whispers of possibility, the warmth of something that could be love. There had been moments of connection, brief flashes of something real, but they had always faded as if love was a dream I couldn't hold onto, a reflection I couldn't catch. Yet, there was this unshakable hope that one day, the fog would lift, and I would find the love I had always longed for—clear, undeniable, and right in front of me.

But until then, I had been left to wander through the haze, knowing that every step, every effort was part of the search. The fog had obscured my path, blurred my vision, but it hadn't stopped me from hoping, from believing that love was out there, waiting to be found. It was that hope that had kept me moving forward, even when the world around me felt like it was veiled in uncertainty.

Reading To Be a Poem had shifted something inside me, a transformation I couldn't explain. There had been something about the way the words spoke to me, about the longing woven through the verses, that had awakened a deeper sense of reflection within me. Those days, I often found my thoughts drifting toward love more than anything else, like a soft current pulling me away from the noise and rush of the everyday. It was as if the words had reminded me of a truth I had buried beneath layers of distraction—a truth that love was not just something to seek, but something that shaped us, something that should be felt in every breath, every moment.

I had always thought about love, of course, but after reading that book, it felt different. It was no longer just a distant dream or an abstract idea. Now, love seemed like a living, breathing thing in my mind—something that had weight, something that demanded attention. I thought about what it meant to truly love and be loved, the kind of love that didn't just fill a space but transformed it, that didn't just heal wounds but prevented them from being made in the first place. The idea of being someone's poem—their every thought and feeling etched into the words of their life—had become something I couldn't stop contemplating. It was a beautiful thought, but also a heavy one. Could love really be that pure? That consuming? And if so, was I ready to give myself fully to it?

As I mulled over those thoughts, love started to feel less like something to chase and more like something to embrace, something that required patience, understanding, and vulnerability. I realised that I had spent so much time searching for a love that met my expectations, but perhaps love wasn't something that could be found so easily. Maybe it was something that needed to be nurtured, built slowly, piece by piece. It made me more aware of the small moments of connection that happened every day, of the quiet ways people loved one another, even when they didn't realise it.

I found myself wondering if I would ever find a love that felt like home, a love that wrapped around me like the words of a poem—soothing and constant. But more than that, I wondered if I was ready to open my heart enough to let love in, to let it fill the spaces I had kept locked away for so long.

As I neared the end of the book, the author explained how she was tired of loving and just wanted to be loved instead. That sentiment lingered in my mind like an unanswered question.

*So, I wish to be a poem—a carefully crafted verse that lingers in someone's heart, timeless and unforgettable. Not just any poem, but one that speaks to the very soul, something that can be felt in the quiet spaces between breaths, in the unspoken words that hang in the air. I long to be the kind of poem that is written not just with ink, but with the essence of life itself—the beauty and the pain, the joy and the sorrow, all woven together in a way that no one could ever forget.*

*I wish to be the lines that someone recites in their lonely moments, when they are lost in thought, or when the weight of the world becomes too heavy. I want to be the words that bring comfort, that make someone feel understood, that reassure them that they are not alone in this vast, sometimes unforgiving world. I want to be the poem that makes them smile when they least expect it, the one that gives them strength when they're feeling weak.*

*But it's not just about being heard or remembered. I want to be a poem that touches the heart in a way that nothing else can. I want my presence to be felt, to be the gentle reminder that love and beauty can be found in the smallest moments. I want to be the words that are carried through time, not just for what they say, but for the way they make someone feel—alive, seen, cherished.*

*And perhaps, in wanting to be a poem, I am also hoping to be understood, to be something that resonates with someone in a way that is profound and lasting. Maybe I wish to be a poem because, like a well-written verse, I too long for connection—something deep, something that lingers long after the moment has passed. I want to be more than just fleeting moments or passing conversations. I want to be something eternal, something that stays with them, long after they turn the page.*

As I turned the final page, a strange mix of satisfaction and longing settled over me. The story had taken me on a journey I hadn't expected, and now, it was over, leaving behind a void that only a truly remarkable book can create. I closed it gently, almost reverently, and let my fingers trail over the cover. My eyes drifted to the author's name, etched in bold letters beneath the title: Seraphine Mitchell. I stared at the name for a moment, letting it sink in, wondering what kind of mind could create something so captivating.

For a moment, I sat there, the name echoing in my thoughts as if trying to grasp some deeper connection to the person who had given life to such a beautiful world. Her words stayed with me long after the book closed. They haunted me, comforted me, and called me to write back.

# 4
## Alasdair

It began without intention, like a quiet murmur growing louder with every passing thought. One moment, I was staring at the pages of her book, my mind still reeling from the emotions it had stirred. The next, I was at my desk, pen in hand, as if compelled by something far greater than myself. I wasn't writing just another story; I was beginning a reply to hers. Not a critique, not an analysis—but something far more personal. A letter. A letter from me to her, written in the only way I knew how: as a book.

I told myself it was absurd. She would never read it, would never even know it existed. And yet, I couldn't stop. There was a pull I couldn't explain, an urge to reach out across the invisible distance between us and respond to the questions her words had planted in my mind. Her book had spoken to something buried deep within me, and now it was as though I had no choice but to answer.

Each word I wrote felt like I was peeling back layers of my soul, uncovering parts of myself I hadn't known were hidden. Her story had touched places I had long kept locked away, and with every sentence, I felt as though I was opening those doors, letting her see the truths I had buried. The book wasn't just a reply to hers—it was a mirror reflecting everything I had felt but never expressed, everything I had longed for but never dared to ask.

Even as I wrote, a part of me questioned why I was doing it. Was it foolish? Was it pointless? Perhaps. But the act of writing felt like a conversation I desperately needed to have. Her book had reached me in a way nothing else ever had, and now, my words felt like a way to bridge the silence, to tell her the things I couldn't say aloud: I see you. I hear you. I understand.

And though I knew this letter would likely remain unread, gathering dust on a shelf or hidden away in a drawer, it didn't matter. It was a dialogue she might never hear, but one I needed to have, if only for myself.

It took me around four months to complete the book. Four months of pouring every thought, every feeling, and every ounce of myself into those pages. It wasn't just a book—it was my letter, my answer, my connection to a stranger who would likely never know I existed. Once it was done, I felt both elated and empty, like I had given away a piece of my soul. But the work wasn't finished. The next step was harder—finding someone willing to give my book a chance.

As usual, I began the gruelling process of looking for publishers. I sent query after query, knocked on countless doors, only to be met with rejection. Months passed, and my hope began to waver. The words "not a good fit" or "unfortunately, we must decline" became so familiar that they felt like a permanent echo in my head. Yet, I couldn't bring myself to give up. This wasn't just another story to me; it was my heart, laid bare. My book, my letter, needed to be seen.

That day, I tried again. This time, I headed to a small, relatively unknown publishing house. It wasn't one of the prestigious ones I had dreamed about when I first started writing, but by then, I was less concerned about the name and more about finding someone who would listen. As I walked through their modest doors, manuscript clutched tightly in my hands, I told myself that this time would be different. I wouldn't leave until they saw it. Until someone saw it.

I sat in the waiting area, the thin cushion of the chair doing little to make the wait comfortable. I had grown too used to waiting. It was almost second nature by then, sitting with my hopes bundled up in a stack of papers, wishing for the impossible. Every day, I had longed for someone to not just skim through my manuscript, but to really see it—to understand the words I had written. But every time, it was ignored, pushed aside like a paper that didn't matter.

This place felt different, though. It was smaller and somehow less intimidating. When the editor finally called me in, I handed him my manuscript with a mix of hope and resignation. He took it, his expression unreadable, and flipped open the first page.

At first, I braced myself for the usual signs of disinterest—a bored glance, a quick skim through the first few lines before setting it down. But something strange happened. He didn't skim. He read. His eyes widened slightly, and he leaned forward, holding the pages as though they were heavier than they looked. His brow furrowed, not with confusion but with focus, and when he finally looked up at me, his expression was somewhere between astonishment and curiosity.

"What have you written?" he asked, his voice low, almost reverent.

I was taken aback by the question. It wasn't dismissive or skeptical like the others I had heard. It was genuine, almost awed, as if he had stumbled upon something unexpected. For a moment, I didn't know how to respond.

"It's…" I paused, taking a deep breath before continuing. "It's a letter. A letter to someone I've never met. It's personal."

He didn't say anything immediately, just looked back down at the manuscript, flipping through a few more pages. "This," he said, tapping the paper, "this isn't just a book. It's raw. It's… alive. I've never seen anything like it."

My nerves began to tangle up, a mix of hope and disbelief swirling within me. "Does that mean… you'll consider it?"

He leaned back in his chair, still holding the manuscript. "Consider it? I'd be a fool not to. Let me finish reading it, but I'll tell you this now—I think you've got something here. Something special."

His words hit me all at once, and for the first time in months, I felt like maybe that letter of mine might find its way into the world.

I couldn't speak. His words hung in the air, sinking into me like the first rays of sunlight after a long, stormy night. I had spent so long chasing this moment, dreaming of it, but now that it was here, I didn't know how to react. Part of me wanted to leap out of my chair and celebrate, but another part hesitated, afraid to believe it could be real.

He returned to the manuscript, flipping through the pages with a kind of intensity that made me feel exposed, as though he wasn't just reading the words but seeing into me. The silence stretched on, but it wasn't the oppressive kind I was used to. This silence felt alive, filled with possibility.

After what felt like an eternity, he looked up again. "Tell me something," he said, setting the manuscript down. "Did you write this for someone specific?"

I hesitated, unsure how much to reveal. "Yes," I admitted. "But… they'll probably never read it."

He nodded slowly as if he understood. "That's what makes it so powerful. It's not written to impress or entertain. It's written for someone, and that makes it real." He tapped the manuscript again. "I want to take this to the team. We're a small house, but we care about stories like this. Stories that matter. If they feel the same way I do, we'll move forward."

My breath caught. "You mean… you want to publish it?"

He smiled, a small but genuine smile that felt like a lifeline. "I can't promise anything yet, but yes. I think we can make this happen."

The relief that washed over me was almost overwhelming. For months, I had faced nothing but rejection, doors slamming in my face before I could even explain myself. And now, here was someone who not only saw my work but believed in it.

"Thank you," I managed to say, my voice shaky. "Thank you for giving it a chance."

He stood, extending his hand. "Don't thank me yet. Let's see where this goes. But I'll be in touch soon. For now, take a deep breath. You've earned it."

As I left the office, manuscript no longer in my hands, I felt lighter than I had in months. The weight of uncertainty wasn't entirely gone, but for the first time, it didn't feel unbearable. I stepped out into the cool evening air, the faint glow of streetlights reflecting the flicker of hope inside me.

This wasn't just a step forward—it was the beginning of something new. Something real. My letter, my book, might finally find its voice in the world. As I walked down the quiet street, I couldn't help but smile, the possibility of what lay ahead igniting something I hadn't felt in a long time: belief in myself.

## 5
## Seraphine

Life had been loud, so loud that I failed to hear my own voice.

The clamour began the moment I woke up. My phone buzzed incessantly on the nightstand—emails from my publisher, reminders from my assistant, and messages from readers who had somehow managed to find my number. I squinted at the screen, debating whether to answer or throw the device out the window. The thought had been tempting.

I rolled out of bed, already dreading the day ahead. My schedule stared back at me from the planner on the desk, each line filled with meetings, deadlines, and obligations I neither had the time nor the energy to fulfil. Somewhere in all that chaos, I was supposed to write. That was the irony of being a famous author—once you "made it," you had less time to do the very thing that got you there.

The coffee machine had been my only solace. As I waited for it to brew, I glanced at the half-finished manuscript sitting on my desk.

It was due in three weeks, and I hadn't written a single word in days. Not for lack of trying, but because my mind felt like it had been drowned in noise. The demands, the expectations, the endless chatter—they had all but silenced the voice I used to trust so deeply.

By the time I had downed my coffee, my day was already in full swing. A car arrived to take me to a radio interview. The host gushed about how much they loved my latest book, and I plastered on a smile, thanking them for their kind words while secretly wondering if they had actually read it. The questions were predictable: "What inspires you?" "How do you deal with writer's block?" "What's next for you?" I answered them on autopilot, my responses so rehearsed they had lost all meaning.

Lunch had been a blur of networking with people I barely knew, discussing collaborations and projects I didn't have time for. By the time I returned home, it was late afternoon, and I was exhausted. Yet, the manuscript still sat there, waiting. The characters were calling to me, their stories begging to be told, but I couldn't seem to hear them over the din of everything else.

I tried anyway. I sat down, fingers hovering over the keyboard, staring at the blinking cursor. Nothing came. My mind was too cluttered, my thoughts too scattered. The words I used to pull so easily from the depths of my soul felt out of reach, like they had been buried under the weight of expectations.

The evening was no quieter. There was a book signing at a packed bookstore, followed by a dinner event with industry professionals. By the time I got home, it was almost midnight, and my body felt like it had been wrung out and left to dry.

I sat on the edge of my bed, staring out the window at the city lights. Life had been loud, so loud that I wondered if I'd ever find serenity again. But as tired as I was, I knew I'd wake up the next day and do it all over again. Because somewhere in all that chaos was a tiny, flickering hope: the hope that I'd find my voice again, that I'd remember why I had started this journey in the first place.

But through it all, I never failed to make time for my fiancé. In a life so consumed by words, deadlines, and applause that often felt hollow, he had been the only constant I couldn't bring myself to let go of, even though I probably should have. Love, for me, had always been about persistence, about holding on through the storms. But with him, I had started to wonder if I was holding on to an illusion—something that had once existed or maybe never did.

He hadn't made it easy. If anything, he actively pushed me away. His silences had been louder than my applause; his indifference had been sharper than any rejection letter. Yet, I still went to him. I still found myself standing outside his door with takeout boxes or a bottle of wine, hoping he'd let me in. Sometimes he did, sometimes he didn't, but even when he did, I could feel the distance in the air between us.

Last week, I showed up unannounced after a particularly exhausting book signing. I needed him that night—just his presence, his calm. He opened the door, his face unreadable as usual.

"You should've called," he said, stepping aside to let me in but not looking at me.

"I thought we were past the need for formalities," I replied lightly, trying to mask the ache his coldness always stirs in me.

He didn't answer, just walked back to the couch where a movie played on mute. I sat beside him, close enough to feel his warmth but not enough to bridge the gap that was always there.

"I missed you," I said softly, my eyes on the screen.

He didn't respond, didn't even turn to look at me. His silence was deafening, and yet, I stayed.

It was always like this—me reaching out, him retreating further. And still, I couldn't stop. I told myself it's because love is about effort, about fighting for what matters. But deep down, I knew it was more than that. It was fear. Fear of what it would mean to let go. Fear of admitting that the love I felt wasn't enough to make him stay.

Some nights, I lay awake next to him, his back turned to me, and wondered what I was doing. Why did I keep pouring myself into someone who couldn't even offer me a fraction of what I gave? Why did I write stories about love that heals, love that transforms, when I was living a love that was tearing me apart piece by piece?

But then, there were moments—small, fleeting moments that kept me tethered. Like the way he absentmindedly brushed my hair out of my face when he thought I was asleep. Or the time he showed up to my book launch, standing in the back, his hands shoved in his pockets, as if he didn't want me to know he was there. Those moments convinced me there was something still worth fighting for.

So, I went to him. I stayed. I made time, even when it felt like I was chasing a shadow. Because I couldn't let go of the hope that one day, he'd stop pushing me away. That one day, he'd see me—not as an obligation, not as someone who clings too tightly, but as the person who had always chosen him, no matter how much it hurt.

The next day, a Sunday, I decided to cancel all my meetings. My mind felt too cluttered to engage with anyone, and besides, I needed the day for myself—to think, to breathe, and to do some much-needed research for my ongoing book. Inspiration had been scarce lately, and I knew just the place to find it: the little neighbourhood bookstore a few blocks away.

The bookstore wasn't anything grand or trendy. It was small and tucked between a coffee shop and a dry cleaner, the kind of place you might miss if you weren't paying attention. But it had charm, and more importantly, it held treasures—books by both small and big authors, obscure titles you couldn't find in chain stores. It was a good place to get lost, to discover something unexpected, and that's exactly what I needed.

I pushed open the door, and the familiar faint scent of old paper and polished wood filled my nose, instantly calming me. The bell above the door jingled, followed by the cranky sound of the heavy door shutting behind me. It felt like stepping into another world, one where time moved slower.

The owner looked up from his stool behind the counter. He was old—probably older than all the books lining the shelves and always wore the same pair of round glasses that rested precariously on the tip of his nose. His warm smile spread across his face as he saw me.

"Welcome, miss. Long time no see," he said in a gravelly voice.

I returned his smile, comforted by his familiarity. "How have you been?" I asked.

"Oh, just living, as usual," he replied with a shrug, his eyes twinkling. It was the kind of response that was neither optimistic nor pessimistic. Just honest.

I nodded, understanding the sentiment, and began weaving through the aisles. Each shelf was crammed with books, their spines a mosaic of faded colours and peeling labels. I ran my fingers lightly over the edges as I walked, the texture of worn paper and fabric oddly soothing.

Carefully, I examined each section, hoping to find something that sparked the inspiration I had been searching for. My next book was turning out to be quite philosophical—a departure from my usual style—and I needed something that resonated, something to guide my scattered thoughts.

As I browsed, I heard the faint creak of the floorboards behind me. "May I help you?" the owner asked, his voice kind.

I turned to him, holding a book I had just picked up. Its cover was worn, the title barely legible. "No, no, it's fine," I said, smiling politely. "I can find it on my own."

He nodded, his expression understanding. "Alright, dear. Just let me know if you need anything."

I watched as he slowly retreated to his stool behind the counter, his movements deliberate and unhurried, like a man who had lived long enough to understand the value of taking his time.

I turned back to the shelves, letting my eyes wander over the rows of books. Philosophy, human nature, the mysteries of life—these were the themes I was drawn to that day. I pulled out one book, then another, flipping through pages, reading snippets here and there. Some caught my attention more than others. A phrase, a question, or a single word could linger in my mind, sparking ideas.

The store was quiet, save for the occasional sound of pages turning and the distant hum of the street outside. It was the kind of quiet that felt sacred, a silence that invited thought rather than stifling it.

As I moved along the aisles, my fingers brushed over the spines of countless books, some familiar, others completely foreign. I was immersed in my search, letting my mind drift and wander when something caught my eye.

It was a book that stood out among the worn and dusty volumes surrounding it. Unlike the others, with their faded covers and peeling edges, this one looked almost new, as though it had been waiting untouched for someone to notice it. The title glimmered faintly in gold letters: To Be a Poet.

I paused, squinting slightly to make sure I had read it right. The words felt oddly familiar, stirring something deep within me. I reached for the book, pulling it carefully from its place on the shelf. The cover was simple yet striking—a deep emerald green with the title embossed in gold. No images, no excessive design, just those four words that felt as though they were speaking directly to me.

A small smile tugged at the corners of my lips, half astonishment, half curiosity. "Why is this so similar to mine?" I murmured under my breath.

I flipped it over to check the author's name. There, in small, elegant print, it read: Alasdair Davies.

I frowned slightly, trying to place the name. "Alasdair Davies?" I whispered to myself. "Never heard of him before..." My thoughts wandered as I turned the book over in my hands, examining it more closely. The pages were crisp, the binding firm—this wasn't an old relic like many of the books in the store. It was fresh, untouched, as though it had been waiting for me to find it.

The title intrigued me, almost as if it was challenging me. I couldn't help but feel a strange pull toward it, a sense of connection I couldn't quite explain. The words felt personal, as if they were meant for me—or from me.

Without a second thought, I clutched the book to my chest. "I'll take this one," I said aloud, more to myself than to the store's owner.

The sound of my voice must have caught his attention because, moments later, I heard his slow, deliberate footsteps approaching. "Ah, good choice," he said, peering at the book in my hands. "That one's new to the collection. Came in just last week."

"Do you know anything about the author?" I asked, unable to hide my curiosity.

The old man shook his head, his glasses sliding down the bridge of his nose. "Not much, I'm afraid. Haven't read it yet myself. But you're the first to pick it up, so perhaps it was waiting for you."

I laughed softly, though his words sent a little shiver down my spine. "Perhaps," I murmured, my fingers tracing the golden letters on the cover.

As I headed to the counter to pay, I couldn't shake the feeling that this book was significant somehow. It was as though it had found me, rather than the other way around.

The owner rang up my purchase, slipping the book into a simple brown paper bag. "Enjoy, miss. And let me know what you think of it next time you stop by."

"I will," I promised, though I already knew I wouldn't be able to wait long before diving into its pages.

As I left the bookstore, the crisp winter air greeted me, but I barely noticed the cold. My thoughts were entirely consumed by the book in my hands, the weight of it both literal and metaphorical. I couldn't help but wonder what lay within its pages—and why it felt so eerily connected to me.

By the time I reached home, my coffee table was littered with my usual research books, but none of them seemed as important now. With a deep breath, I settled onto the couch, unwrapped the brown paper, and opened *To Be a Poet.* The first page greeted me with an inscription, written in elegant, slanted handwriting:

*To the dreamers who long to become poems themselves, this is for you.*

# 6
# Seraphine

I settled into my comfort corner, the one spot in the room where everything felt right, and flipped the pages. The pages greeted me with a crispness, the kind that promises something fresh yet familiar. It wasn't a heavy book, but there was a certain weight to it, like it held something important between its covers. Something worth discovering. The texture of the pages beneath my fingers felt grounding, each one a quiet invitation to dive deeper into the world the author had created.

*I've always believed that a poet is just someone who's waiting for their own story to be told—but what if my story is still waiting for me to find it?*

The first line felt like a contradiction to everything I had dreamed. I longed to be a poem, a living, breathing piece of art, while he—he wanted to be the poet, the one to shape the words, to write the stories. It was as if our desires were on opposite ends of the spectrum, and yet, both of us were searching for something the other held.

*What if the waiting itself is part of the story? The silent moments of wondering, the restless nights of imagining, and the fleeting glimpses of something profound—these are not empty spaces. They are the preludes, the foundations of a narrative that is slowly unfolding.*

*Perhaps your story isn't hiding from you; perhaps it's revealing itself in fragments, asking you to gather them patiently, to assemble meaning from the chaos. It's in the faces of strangers, in the rain-soaked streets, in the silence after a sigh. It's in the words you have yet to write and the emotions you haven't fully understood.*

*So perhaps the question isn't whether your story is waiting for you, but whether you are ready to embrace it as it comes—unfinished, imperfect, and yet utterly yours. Because to be a poet is not to own a story but to live it, to shape it with your words and your silences, and to trust that even in the waiting, you are exactly where you're meant to be.*

*Now, to the dreamers—you, who carry love like a secret flame, burning quietly within. You have love to give, boundless and pure, but you hesitate to claim it for yourself. You long to be seen, to be held, yet you shy away from the one gaze that matters most: your own.*

*But here's the truth—when you finally turn inward and learn to own that love, to embrace yourself wholly, you'll unlock the clarity you've been searching for. You'll stop chasing shadows, stop reaching for love in places it was never meant to be found.*

*Because love isn't something you find; it's something you recognise. And when you love yourself, you'll see it waiting for you—not in the distance, but in the arms of those who see you as you truly are. You'll realise that the wrong places were never the problem—it was that you didn't know the treasure you already carried within.*

It's strange, isn't it? How words, when laid bare, can feel like a mirror held to your soul, even if they weren't born from your hand. They cut through the clutter, sidestep the masks, and whisper directly to the parts of you that even you sometimes ignore.

My book—My story—was always about finding the love I deserve, the kind that wraps itself around my existence and says, "You are enough." But perhaps, in that search, I stumbled upon something else. Not a reflection of what I lacked, but a reminder of what I hold.

This wasn't just about finding love; it was about becoming it. About realising that the love you seek isn't waiting outside of you, but within you—ready to bloom when you let it. Maybe these words, this moment, was the universe nudging me, saying, I see you. I've always seen you.

I was about to read the rest when my alarm rang—the one I set to remind myself to get ready to meet my fiancé. The sound cut through the silence like a jolt, dragging me from the warmth of my thoughts into the reality of the day ahead.

I closed the book slowly, my thumb tracing the edge of the page as if reluctant to leave its words behind. For a moment, I paused, staring at nothing, feeling an odd heaviness settle in my chest. I tried to brush it off as pre-meeting jitters, the kind that usually came before seeing someone you thought was your forever.

But this time, it was different. I'd felt it for weeks now—an unease I couldn't name but couldn't ignore. Little things. Missed calls, vague excuses, a certain distance that words couldn't bridge. I wanted to believe it was nothing, that love was just going through its inevitable ebb and flow.

Still, a part of me couldn't shake the gnawing doubt. A part of me didn't want to go at all. But I did. I got ready, trying to silence the voice in my head, the one whispering that I might not like what I was walking into.

And I didn't.

When I arrived, the truth was waiting for me—raw, undeniable, and shattering. My fiancé wasn't alone, and the tenderness I'd once believed was meant for me was now being shared with someone else.

At that moment, everything stopped. The world didn't tilt or spin—it simply paused, as if giving me the space to absorb what my heart already knew. The love I'd been searching for wasn't here. It wasn't mine. And maybe it never had been.

I turned and walked away, my mind strangely calm, the book I'd left unfinished now echoing in my thoughts. To the dreamers—you have love within yourself.

I still had that, didn't I? And maybe, just maybe, that was enough for now.

I wanted to confront him, to shout, to demand answers, to break it all off right there. But I couldn't. Our engagement wasn't just about us. It was a promise etched into time, made long before we were even born. It connected two families, tied with threads far stronger than my own will. It wasn't in my hands to untangle them, even as they strangled my heart.

If this had happened before reading the book, I would've accepted it. I would've forced a smile, convinced myself that loving him was enough. That my love alone could carry the weight of what we were supposed to be. I would've stayed silent, happy in my delusion, thinking at least I love him.

But then, something had changed. That book, those words—they had planted something in me. They had taught me that loving someone else began with learning to love myself. And now, my self-respect, fragile but present, refused to let me stay blind. It refused to let me keep loving someone who had broken what I once thought was unbreakable.

In a single moment, all the love, all the respect I had held for him came crashing down, shattering into pieces too small to put back together. I had thought I'd feel anger, maybe even hatred, but all I felt was emptiness—a hollow space where hope used to live.

And yet, I had felt hopeless. Not because I wanted him back—I didn't—but because I was trapped in that promise, in that life that had been chosen for me. I had been stuck between what my heart knew and what my reality demanded.

But deep inside, a voice had stirred, the one that had whispered to me when I read those pages. It had told me that the hopelessness wasn't the end. That even if I couldn't break those chains yet, there was strength in knowing they didn't define me. That loving myself might just have been the first step to finding a way out.

# 7
## Seraphine

"Mom, is there a way to break off the engagement?"

There was a pause, the kind that hangs heavy with disbelief. "Have you lost your mind? What's wrong?"

"Nothing, just asking," I replied, trying to keep my voice steady, but my heart was anything but calm.

"Did you fight?"

"No. We never fight," I said, and then, almost as an afterthought, added, "Or maybe just I never do."

She sighed, a familiar sound that carried years of expectations and worry. "Whatever it is, solve it out. You two are a match made in heaven. Don't ruin it." Her tone left no room for argument, and before I could respond, she cut the call.

I stared at the phone, her words echoing in my mind. A match made in heaven. What a cruel irony. If heaven was built on betrayal, then maybe we were. But I wasn't sure I believed in that kind of heaven anymore.

In our world, love wasn't just between two people; it was a bond that tied families, communities, histories. To break it wasn't just rebellion—it was betrayal. And yet, wasn't I the one being betrayed?

I stood frozen for a moment, caught between the urge to scream and the crushing sense of helplessness. I wanted to tell her everything, to pour out the truth, but the thought of her disappointment stopped me. Would she even believe me? Or would she brush it off, telling me to adjust, as if love were something you could patch like a torn seam?

I sank into the nearest chair, the tears I'd been holding back finally spilling over. My love, my respect for him—it was gone, shattered. But what was left of me? Did I have enough strength to fight for myself when even my own mother couldn't see my pain?

My eyes fell on the book resting on the coffee table, its cover catching the faint light of the setting sun. It felt like it was waiting for me, like it knew I'd come back to it. I walked over to the couch, my hands trembling slightly, and picked it up.

I opened it to where I'd left off, and my eyes landed on the words as if they'd been written just for this moment:

Hurts, right? But love shouldn't hurt like this.

The words hit me like a truth I had been avoiding. My breath caught in my throat as I reread the sentence, over and over, until it felt burned into my mind. It was as though the book knew exactly what I was feeling—the ache, the betrayal, the hollow emptiness that came with realising you've given your heart to someone who didn't deserve it.

Love wasn't supposed to feel like this. It wasn't supposed to make you question your worth or leave you wondering if you were asking for too much by wanting loyalty, respect, and care.

I ran my fingers across the page, as if touching the words would make them more real, more mine. For so long, I had believed that love was about endurance—about staying, even when it hurt, about giving, even when it left you empty. But now, these words were telling me otherwise.

I closed my eyes, letting the book rest in my lap, and whispered, almost to myself, "Then why does it?"

The answer wasn't in the book. It was in me. Because I had let it. I had allowed myself to believe that this pain was normal, that it was part of love. But it wasn't. Love wasn't supposed to destroy you. It was supposed to build you up.

But then again, I was stuck. Stuck in a world of lies, where one deceit led to another, and covering up those lies had become second nature not just for him, but for me too. I had lied to myself, hadn't I? Pretending everything was fine, pretending that love alone could hold together something already broken.

I was trapped in a web I didn't weave but had willingly stepped into, convincing myself that it was my duty to stay. To preserve the illusion, for the sake of families, traditions, and expectations that weren't even mine to carry.

But the worst part wasn't his lies; it was mine. The lies I told myself every day—that it would get better, that I could fix this, that my love was enough to fill the chasm between us. And now, as I sat there, staring at the book in my lap, I felt the weight of those lies pressing down on me, heavier than ever.

The truth was suffocating, yet liberating. I had been complicit in my own entrapment, and now that I saw it clearly, I didn't know how to escape. Even if I wanted to break free, where would I go? How would I untangle myself from the expectations and obligations that held me in place?

I closed the book and leaned back, staring at the ceiling as if it held the answers. I wanted to believe that I had the strength to choose myself, to walk away, to stop covering up his lies and my own. But every time I thought about it, I felt that familiar pull of hopelessness, the fear of what lay beyond this mess.

"Oh Alasdair…" I whispered, tracing his name on the book. "Every time I open your pages, I wonder if I'm reading you or if you're reading me."

# 8
# Seraphine

Every day, I set aside fifteen minutes for the book. Just fifteen, I told myself, but somehow, those minutes always stretched into thirty, sometimes even more. It had been hard to stop once I started. The words had a way of pulling me in, like they'd been waiting for me all along.

It was strange how something could feel so different, yet so familiar. The sentences, the thoughts—they had been like a mirror, reflecting parts of me I hadn't known I was ready to see. Each page felt like a conversation, one I'd been avoiding but desperately needed to have.

Some passages felt like they were written just for me, as if the author knew my struggles, my doubts, my longing for something more. And yet, there had been a universality in them, a reminder that pain and growth, love and loss, weren't mine alone.

Every time I closed the book, I felt a little lighter and a little heavier all at once. Lighter because it had given me hope, heavier because it had left me with truths I couldn't ignore. And so, every day, I returned to it—not just to read but to understand, to piece together the fragments of myself that I'd been too afraid to face.

Soon, I found myself nearing the end of the book, and my heart began to race with a mix of anticipation and dread. Each turned page felt heavier than the last, as if the words were carrying me toward something inevitable.

I had grown so attached to its voice, its rhythm, its way of pulling apart my defences. This book wasn't just something I read. It was something that had started to reshape me, one sentence at a time.

But now, as the pages grew thinner, I felt an ache I couldn't explain. What would I do when it ended? When there were no more words to hold my hand through this storm, no more passages to reflect the feelings I couldn't articulate?

I slowed down, reading each word carefully, savouring them, even as I felt the pull to race to the finish. It was strange—part of me wanted to know how it ended, but another part feared that the ending might leave me with more questions than answers.

The book had been a companion, a guide, a mirror. And soon, it would be over. What would that mean for me? Would I finally be ready to face my truth without it? Or would I feel lost, searching for another anchor in a sea of uncertainty?

With every page, my heart beat faster, and yet, I kept going. Because as much as I feared the ending, I also knew that some stories—like mine—don't really end. They just shift, pushing you forward into the next chapter of your life.

And finally, I reached the end.

So, I wish to be a poet. To find my poem—the one that's been waiting for me, hiding between the lines of my life, buried in the stillness I've been too afraid to face.

I want to embrace it, not just as words on a page, but as truth woven into the fabric of who I am. I want to let it spill out of me, raw and unfiltered, capturing the moments I've ignored, the emotions I've denied, and the dreams I've kept locked away.

My poem isn't perfect. It won't rhyme in all the right places or flow without hesitation. It will stumble, pause, and bleed, just as I have. It will carry the weight of my heartbreaks and my triumphs, my failures and my resilience.

But that's what makes it mine. That's what makes it real.

Being a poet isn't about crafting something flawless; it's about capturing the truth, even when it's messy, even when it hurts. It's about daring to see yourself in every stanza, every metaphor, and knowing that even the broken lines are part of the story.

So I'll search for my poem, not in someone else's shadow but in the light I'm learning to find within myself. And when I find it, I'll embrace it—not just as a reflection of who I was, but as a promise of who I can become.

The last words echoed through my head, reverberating like a distant thunderstorm that refused to fade. As I read them, it felt like the book was holding my breath, like it had saved its most profound truth for the very end.

And then, I stopped reading.

My heart started racing, pounding so hard it felt like it might burst out of my chest. The silence that followed was deafening, filled only with the sound of my breathing.

It was over. The book had ended, but something in me had only just begun.

I stared at the closed cover in my lap, unable to let it go. It felt like saying goodbye to a friend who had seen me at my most vulnerable, who had shown me parts of myself I didn't even know existed. I had come to this book looking for answers, but instead, it had handed me a mirror.

I placed the book down gently, my fingers trembling. My thoughts were a whirlwind, my emotions raw and unguarded. For the first time in a long time, I wasn't afraid to feel them.

Those words had left a mark on me, one I couldn't erase even if I wanted to. And as I sat there, my heart racing and my mind restless, I realised that maybe this was the beginning of something new. Something honest. Something mine.

# 9
## Alasdair

It had been six months since my book was published, and I'd had only two sales. Two. One of which was bought by Albert—sweet, loyal Albert, who would probably have bought a bag of air if I'd told him I needed the support.

I wouldn't lie; it stung. I had poured my heart into that book, each page a piece of my soul, but the world had barely noticed. Still, at least it had been published. That was something, right? A small victory in itself, though it had felt more like a consolation prize on most days.

To keep my mind off the disappointment, I immersed myself in Seraphine Mitchell's books. I'd bought them all, one after another, devouring them like they were a lifeline. They hadn't been my usual kind of reads, but every one of them had left me feeling ecstatic.

Her stories had this way of reaching into the corners of your soul. They didn't just entertain—they unraveled me, forcing me to look at myself in ways I'd rather not. And maybe that was why I couldn't stop reading them. Because in some strange way, they reminded me of why I wanted to write in the first place.

I wondered if her first book had struggled too, if she'd spent nights staring at a blank sales report, wondering if her words would ever find their audience. Had she felt this kind of disappointment? Or had her journey been as seamless as her prose?

Either way, her books kept me going. They reminded me that writing wasn't just about the sales or the recognition—it was about connection. And maybe my book hadn't found its readers yet. But it would. At least, that was what I told myself as I turned the pages of her work, hoping that one day, someone would feel about my words the way I felt about hers.

I even did a lot of research on her, desperate to know more about the person behind the words that had shaken my soul.

"Seraphine Mitchell is a bestselling Scottish author who made her debut at the age of seventeen. Her popular books include Loveless Nights, To Be a Poem, and others," every search seemed to say the same thing, over and over.

And that was it. That's all I found. No in-depth articles about her life or process—just those brief, impersonal sentences. I even found a few radio interviews but they didn't contain anything personal. All she said was—"What inspires me? I don't know, maybe life?"

It was frustrating and fascinating all at once. In a world where everything and everyone feels overexposed, she was a mystery.

I couldn't help but wonder: who was she, really? What had inspired her to write the way she did, to weave words that cut so deeply and yet felt so healing? How did she capture emotions so real, as if she had lived every possible version of love and loss?

The fact that she debuted at seventeen made it all the more intriguing. What kind of seventeen-year-old has the wisdom to write like that? At seventeen, I could barely figure out who I was, let alone pour my soul onto paper for the world to see.

Part of me wanted to keep searching, to dig deeper until I uncovered some hidden detail about her life. But another part of me respected her silence. Maybe her work spoke for her, and that was enough. Maybe the mystery was part of the magic.

Still, I couldn't shake the feeling that there was more to her than those polished, vague lines in her biography. And as I read her books late into the night, I found myself wondering—not just about her stories, but about her. Who she was. Who she might have been. And why her words felt like they were meant just for me.

A few months later, her new book was released, and it was as if the entire city had come alive. The bookstore was buzzing with energy on the day of the launch, a restless crowd spilling out onto the sidewalk. I had never seen anything like it—people clutching her previous books, speaking in hushed tones as if preparing for a sacred ritual.

I joined the queue, stretching so far down the street that it felt like an eternity before I even stepped inside. The excitement was palpable, infectious, as if every person there had been touched by her words in some deeply personal way. I waited for hours, shuffling forward inch by inch, feeling both the impatience of wanting the book in my hands and the strange camaraderie of standing among so many others who shared the same reverence for her work.

When I finally held it, I felt a rush of something I couldn't explain—relief, awe, anticipation. The cover was simple yet haunting, her name printed boldly across the top as if the mere mention of it carried weight. I clutched it close, not wanting to let go, as though it was more than a book—it was a piece of her, a piece of whatever magic she poured into her words.

The power she holds is insane. To draw so many people together, to create this collective hunger for her stories, her thoughts—it was almost otherworldly. And as I walked out of the store with her latest masterpiece in hand, I realised that power wasn't just in her words. It was in her ability to make people feel seen, to make them believe that their own stories mattered too.

And now, holding her new book, I couldn't wait to see what pieces of myself I might discover this time.

Not being able to contain my excitement, I ripped open the packaging on the bus itself. The fresh scent of new pages filled the air as I opened the book, my fingers trembling just a little. I was surrounded by people, and the hum of the city outside, but none of it seemed to matter. At that moment, all I could focus on was the words that lay ahead, waiting for me to dive in.

The title shined bright— My Poet.

Multiple questions rose in my mind. Did she already find her poet? Did she find the love she was looking for? All I could think was how happy I'd be to know that she got what she always dreamed of. But a small part of me wanted to be her dream, her very own poet.

As I started reading, I noticed that the book seemed more like a question rather than an answer to her previous one.

*Sometimes I wonder—are you the poet I've been searching for?*

*But then I remind myself: you're too far away. Too untouchable. Too hidden in the shadows of the unknown.*

*Your words reach me like the rays of the morning sun, yet you remain just out of reach, like a star I can only admire but never hold. I've combed through everything I could find about you, hoping for some clue, some glimpse of the person behind the poetry, but all I've found are echoes. Fragments. Just enough to keep me wondering, but never enough to truly know.*

*You feel like a paradox—so present in your work, yet so absent from the world. Sometimes it frustrates me, this distance. Other times, I think it's what makes your words so powerful. You've carved yourself into the lines, left pieces of your soul in every stanza, and yet you've remained untouched by the chaos of being known.*

*And maybe that's what makes you the poet I've been looking for. Someone who doesn't just write, but lives in their poetry, someone who chooses to be felt rather than seen.*

*But even as your words pull me closer, I can't help but feel the gap between us. A chasm filled with questions, with longing, with the ache of never knowing if you're as real as the stories you tell—or if I've made you into something more in my mind.*

This was for someone. Definitely someone. My heart skipped a beat as I read the words, as if the world around me experienced a sudden pause. She didn't know me. Then why did it feel like all her words were directed towards me only? If love had a language, it would sound like this— words you didn't write for me, and yet somehow, they belong to me.

"You wrote like someone was listening. I read like someone had been waiting," I murmured, my fingertips tracing her name on the cover, lingering over the letters as if they might reveal something more. Seraphine Mitchell. A name that had become both a mystery and a comfort to me.

The weight of the book in my lap felt heavier than it should, like it carried more than just words—like it held pieces of her soul, pieces she had willingly given to whoever cared to look. I wondered if she knew how deeply those words could burrow, how they could nestle into someone's heart and refuse to leave.

As the bus jostled forward, I closed my eyes for a moment, her words echoing in my mind. I could almost picture her, somewhere far away, writing these lines with the same intensity I now felt while reading them. Did she imagine someone like me—a stranger, lost in the folds of her thoughts, feeling seen for the first time?

I opened the book again, unable to resist the pull of her words. And as I read, a quiet thought surfaced, one I wasn't ready to admit aloud: Maybe I've been waiting for this my entire life.

This book felt less like a story and more like a question—an endless string of thoughts she had tossed into the universe, waiting for someone to catch them. So, I sat down with a notepad.

With every question she posed, I jotted down an answer, my pen moving as if guided by something beyond me. Her words felt alive, sparking something within me. I wasn't just reading anymore; I was responding, as if we were in a silent dialogue.

And as I wrote, I couldn't shake the feeling that this wasn't a one-sided effort. It was as if the universe was conspiring, weaving invisible threads to carry my words back to her. I didn't know how or when, but I believed, with certainty, that my answers would find their way to her.

Perhaps she was waiting, too, just as I had been—waiting for a voice to echo back.

*Will I ever truly find you?*

"Maybe I never met you, but between the lines, where stories live and souls meet, I found you." I answered.

*If you're still finding your poem, how are you a poet?*

## 10

# Seraphine

A busy Sunday, yet I made time to run to the bookstore, the one I always found myself wandering into when my thoughts felt too loud.

"Is there any new book?" I asked, slightly out of breath from the walk.

"Yes, dear," the shopkeeper replied with a kind smile. My heart jumped with excitement as he rummaged through a cardboard box stacked behind the counter. He pulled out a shiny hardcover and handed it to me.

I smiled as I took it, turning it over in my hands, admiring the fresh scent of ink and the glossy cover. "Venessa Cole," it read in bold, elegant letters.

"Not this, sir," I said, placing it gently back on the counter. "I meant any new book by Alasdair Davies? The one I bought last time."

"Oh… not yet," he replied, his voice tinged with apology.

Disappointment crept into my chest, but I masked it with a polite nod. "Alright. Let me know when it arrives."

As I turned to leave, the shopkeeper added, "You really do love his work, don't you?"

I paused, my hand resting on the doorframe. "It's not just his work," I said softly, more to myself than to him. "It's the way he writes. Like he's been through what I'm feeling. Like his words were waiting for me before I even knew I needed them."

The shopkeeper smiled knowingly, but I was already stepping back into the busy street, the world bustling around me.

I walked home slowly, lost in thought. I wondered why his books had such a hold on me. Was it the way he seemed to ask questions I was too afraid to ask myself? Or was it because his words felt like answers to something I couldn't even name?

Either way, I knew I'd return next week, hoping for a new book, a new conversation, a new reason to feel seen.

As I unlocked my front door and stepped inside, the emptiness of the apartment greeted me. I set my bag down, glancing at the small pile of books on my coffee table. At the very top was To Be a Poet by Alasdair Davies, its corners worn from being read and reread.

I picked it up, flipping through the pages until I found the underlined passage I always returned to: The hardest part isn't finding the words—it's letting yourself believe they were meant for you.

The following week, I found myself back at the bookstore. My footsteps were lighter this time, as if my heart had already convinced me that today would be different. That today, his book would be waiting for me.

But as soon as the shopkeeper met my hopeful gaze, his apologetic smile told me everything I needed to know.

"Not yet," he said gently, before I could even ask.

I nodded, offering a small, resigned smile. "It's alright," I murmured, though it wasn't.

As I left, the disappointment sat heavier in my chest. Yet, a stubborn part of me clung to hope. Next week, I thought. It has to be next week.

But it wasn't.

I returned the following week, and the week after that, and again, each time walking through the familiar door only to leave with empty hands. The shopkeeper started greeting me with a knowing shake of his head before I could even speak. He didn't need to say the words anymore; his expression said enough.

"You're persistent, I'll give you that," he finally said one day, as I lingered by the counter longer than usual.

I chuckled, though it didn't reach my eyes. "I just... feel like I need to read it. Like it's waiting for me somewhere, and I just have to keep showing up."

He studied me for a moment, then leaned forward, lowering his voice as if sharing a secret. "Sometimes, the best books take their time finding their way to you. But when they do, they come when you need them most."

I nodded, his words both comforting and frustrating. As much as I wanted to believe that, the waiting felt endless. The anticipation, the buildup—it was beginning to feel like a cruel game.

Yet, I kept coming back. Week after week, I walked into that little shop, clinging to the hope that one day I would walk out with his new book in my hands. Because for some reason, I felt certain that when it finally arrived, it wouldn't just be a book—it would be something more. Something I needed in ways I couldn't yet explain.

And so, I waited. Not because I had to, but because deep down, I knew the best things in life are the ones worth waiting for.

The following week was chaotic. Meetings piled on top of deadlines, leaving me gasping for air, unable to pause and just breathe. Sunday arrived like a lifeline, but instead of peace, it came with a date with Asher.

I didn't want to go. The thought of sitting across from the man who had betrayed me filled me with dread. But I had to. Was this my fate? To keep pretending, to share a table with someone whose lies I had uncovered?

I didn't get the chance to visit the bookstore all week. By evening, I forced myself to dress up for the dinner date. It was a fancy restaurant—his choice, of course. The kind of place that sparkled too much to feel real.

Silence stretched across the table as we sat down, a hollow chasm neither of us seemed eager to bridge. Finally, he broke it. "How have you been?"

"Great," I replied flatly, sipping my wine.

He nodded, then launched into a monologue about his work—how busy he had been, how demanding things were. His words blurred together, a string of excuses I had no energy to parse. I knew where he had really been, the truth sitting between us like a ghost. Still, I pretended not to know, nodding occasionally as I glanced at my wristwatch.

The store closed at 8 p.m., and it was already 7:30.

As his voice droned on, I grabbed my handbag and stood abruptly. "I need to go," I said.

He looked confused. "Where?"

"I have somewhere important to be."

"More important than me?"

"Yes," I said without hesitation.

Before he could respond, I turned and walked away, ignoring his calls as I stepped into the cool evening air. The sun had set, and the city was bathed in the soft glow of streetlights. I quickened my pace, then broke into a run. My heels clicked against the pavement, each step an echo of determination.

My breath came in short gasps as I reached the bookstore just minutes before closing. The shopkeeper was standing at the counter, a knowing smile on his face.

"I knew you'd come," he said warmly.

Something about his words made my heart race. "Is it here?" I asked, my voice trembling.

He nodded and handed me a book wrapped in fresh, crisp paper. The title gleamed under the light. It was here.

Without thinking, I hugged the book to my chest, clutching it as if it were a lifeline. My entire week—the chaos, the betrayal, the disappointment—melted away in that moment.

As I turned to leave, something stopped me. I glanced back at the shopkeeper. "How many copies have been sold? Of this and the previous one?"

His smile faltered slightly, and he looked at me with a mix of sympathy and amusement. "Only you bought them, my dear."

"Only me?" I echoed.

He nodded.

I swallowed hard, my grip tightening around the book. "Give me a few more copies," I said.

He raised an eyebrow. "What will you do with them?"

"Just… to show some support," I replied, my voice firm but tinged with emotion.

He chuckled softly but didn't press further, handing me a few more copies. I paid for them, my heart heavy yet strangely light. As I left the store, I realised it didn't matter if no one else was reading these words. They were meant for me, and that was enough.

I reached home with a rush of excitement, my heart pounding in sync with my steps. I didn't even bother to take off my socks, just dropped onto the bed and opened the book.

Your Poet, the title read, glowing softly under the dim light. In that instant, I was sure. This wasn't just a book—it was a message. A guide. The answers I'd been waiting for were right here in my hands. There was no way this was a coincidence. No way this wasn't meant to be. It was fate.

"Alasdair…" I whispered to the empty room, "We didn't meet by chance. We met through sentences, as though the universe was a librarian, waiting for the right book to fall into my hands."

I opened to the first page, the edges of the paper crisp as I turned them with eager fingers.

The words began with a poem.

*A poet is not the keeper of the final line,*

*But the seeker of truths that quietly shine.*

*The poem is the path, not the end I hold,*

*Each word a step, each silence bold.*


*To search is to write, to wonder is to weave,*

*A poet breathes life into what they believe.*

*So even as I seek, I am what I proclaim—*

*A poet, still finding the heart of my name.*


*And maybe you are my poem—*

*The one I've searched for in every silence,*

*In the spaces between words I couldn't speak,*

*In the echoes of feelings too fragile to name.*


*Maybe you are my poem—*

*Unwritten yet complete,*

*A rhythm I've always felt but never heard,*

*A truth I was too afraid to claim.*

## 11
## Alasdair

Unlike me, she took longer to write. Most likely because her world was full of other responsibilities, and other demands. But that waiting, that anticipation—it wasn't exhausting. It was beautiful. Each day that passed brought me closer to something deeper, something more profound. I knew that when her words finally would reach me, when her next book would land in my hands, the wait would have been worth it.

It was more than just impatience; it was the belief that with every pause, every delay, she had been mending something for me. For us. Somewhere, hidden behind her busy world, she must have read my story, felt my words in the spaces between her own. And every line she had written seemed to speak directly to me. I kept searching her sentences for the thing she didn't say—hoping it was my name. It might sound foolish to some, but to me, it felt too real to dismiss.

I no longer waited with doubt or frustration. I waited with reverence, knowing that when she wrote, she didn't just write for the world. She wrote for me.

As I read the title of the next book, Your Poem, my heart skipped a beat. It felt like the universe whispered my name through the pages, and in that moment, I was certain—this was for me. I gasped, loud enough for people around me to glance over in confusion. My breathing became erratic, and my heart thudded in my chest, as though it, too, was trying to keep up with the rush of realisation.

Not knowing what else to do, I immediately called Albert.

"I think I'm in love, Albert. I'm in love!"

"What? Really? Finally! Who is it?"

"Seraphine! Seraphine Mitchell."

There was a silence on the other end, a long, drawn-out pause that stretched for far too long. Finally, he sighed.

"Seriously?" he asked, his voice now lacking the excitement it once held. "Being a fan is great, but calling that love… that's a bit much, don't you think?"

"If this is what it means to fall in love—finding pieces of yourself in someone else's story—then I've already fallen."

"Alasdair…"

"Wait! Hear me out. Isn't it strange, how a book can feel like the beginning of something that hasn't happened yet? How it can shape your thoughts, tug at your heart, and feel like an unraveling of the soul?"

"Are you trying to joke with me right now?"

"I'm not! I'm serious. It's a strange thing, to love someone in silence. To fall for thoughts on paper and feel as though they were whispered into your ear. It's not like any love I've ever known. It's more like a discovery. Like meeting a part of yourself you never knew existed until it came alive through someone else."

Albert was quiet, and I could almost hear the wheels turning in his mind, processing what I was saying. He wasn't convinced, but somehow, I knew I didn't need him to be. This feeling wasn't for anyone else to understand but me.

I hung up the phone. My pulse raced as I ran home, the cool evening air rushing past me, almost as if it, too, was pushing me toward something I couldn't fully understand. With every step I took, my heart seemed to grow heavier, but in the best way possible—like it was being filled with something I couldn't grasp, but didn't want to let go of.

As I neared my door, the thought hit me again, clearer now than before: I'm not sure what I want more—to meet her, or to keep this perfect mystery between us intact.

The idea of actually meeting Seraphine felt both exhilarating and terrifying. The way her words had become a part of me—it felt almost sacred. What if meeting her shattered this delicate spell? What if she didn't live up to the person I had built up in my mind, the person who had unknowingly shared pieces of herself with me?

But then, the thought of never meeting her, of only loving her through the words she had left behind, felt like I was denying myself something real, something tangible. There was a pull, an undeniable gravity that made me want to close the gap between us. I wanted to know if the warmth I felt when I read her words could translate into something more—something that wasn't confined to the pages of her books.

Yet, as I stood in front of my door, I couldn't shake the feeling that some mysteries were better left unsolved. The distance between us, the untold stories, the unanswered questions—it felt perfect in its own way. Maybe it was better to leave it like this. Maybe this was the only way I could truly love her, through the pages, through the space she had left for me to fill with my own imagination.

But deep down, I knew that one day, I would have to choose. To meet her, or to keep the magic of the unknown.

Reading the book gave my heart both calm and restlessness. I kept turning the pages, afraid of reaching the end—because what happens to us when there are no more words left to be read?

I paused for a moment, the weight of that thought settling over me like a shadow. I couldn't remember the last time I felt so connected to something or someone.

But the closer I got to the end, the more I felt it slipping through my fingers. I wanted to hold onto it, to freeze time, to stay in this liminal space where her words were still mine to uncover. Yet I knew, inevitably, the story would run out.

Would I, too, be left empty when there were no more sentences to trace, no more moments to pause and reread her thoughts? Or would her words echo inside me long after the last page was turned, filling the stillness she'd leave behind?

I kept reading, slower now, each word a bittersweet gift. Because maybe the end wouldn't mean goodbye. What we had was intangible, impossible, and yet it existed—proof that the truest connections begin where eyes don't meet.

## 12
## Seraphine

Today marked three years to the day I first discovered To Be a Poet. Since then, I'd never been the same. I kept writing to him, hoping that he would read, hoping for an answer. And every time, I did receive an answer.

Today, I decided to tell my mother. Face to face. Perfect timing, as she would be visiting me in my apartment.

I paced the living room, straightening cushions that were already aligned, glancing at the clock every few seconds. My palms felt clammy, and the words I had rehearsed in my head suddenly seemed inadequate.

The sound of the doorbell jolted me out of my thoughts. I opened the door, and there she stood, holding a casserole dish and wearing that familiar look of judgment she reserved for my "foolish whims," as she called them.

"Hi, Mom," I said, stepping aside to let her in.

"Seraphine," she said, glancing around. "Your apartment still smells like those scented candles you love so much. Lavender?"

"Vanilla," I corrected, closing the door behind her.

She placed the casserole on the dining table and turned to me. "So, what's this about? You sounded… serious on the phone."

I took a deep breath, the words threatening to choke me. "Mom, I need to tell you something. It's important."

Her eyebrows knitted together, and she folded her arms. "What is it?"

"Mom, I think I'm in love."

"Of course, dear. We all know it."

"No, Mom, not Asher. I'm in love with someone else."

Her eyes flicked to me, her expression softening. "You're confused. It'll pass. Just go meet Asher."

"I'm certain."

"Who is it?" She looked at me, now fully focused.

"Alasdair. Alasdair Davies. My poet."

She raised an eyebrow. "Just tell him you're already engaged."

"I'll break it off," I replied, my voice firm.

She laughed lightly. "Don't joke around like that."

"I'm not."

"Is he from work?"

"No. We met through words. Through stories. Through love."

She stared at me for a long moment. "What do you mean?"

"He's a writer, Mom. We speak through letters—through books."

She blinked, confusion creeping in. "But… you've never met him?"

"No," I said, my voice a little softer now. "But I feel seen. I feel heard."

Her face hardened, and she looked away. "You've completely lost your mind." She shouted, the anger in her voice rising. "You're just pretending to be in love with a ghost, someone who doesn't even know you exist!"

"I'm not pretending," I said, my voice quivering with emotion. "I'm in love."

"No, you're not. You're just confused."

"What are books if not love letters to someone we hope exists?" I asked, my voice shaking.

Without warning, her hand swung across my face, a sharp sting on my cheek. I didn't flinch. I looked at her, my eyes filled with certainty.

"Why?" I shouted. "Why can't you understand?"

She stood there, breathing heavily, and for a moment, I thought she might say something else. But instead, she shook her head.

"You're living in a dream," she muttered. "A dream that isn't real."

I stood still, my heart racing. "Maybe the dream is real. Maybe this is the only truth I've ever known."

Her voice rose, sharp and unyielding. "It's not possible! You can't fall in love with someone you've never met. Love isn't words on a page. It's real. It's tangible. It's two people building a life together—not some fantasy you've created in your head."

I met her gaze, steady, unbroken. "Who decides what love is, Mom? You? Society? The rules we're supposed to follow?" My voice softened, trembling slightly. "Because for me, it's the way his words reach the deepest part of me, the part no one else has ever touched."

"That's not love," she snapped. "That's admiration. It's obsession. Love is Asher, sitting across the table from you, offering you stability and a future."

I shook my head. "Love isn't about proximity. It's about connection. And I've never felt more connected to anyone than I do to him."

"He doesn't even know you exist!" she cried. "How can you be so blind? You're chasing a shadow, Seraphine. A shadow that will never turn into the light you need."

Tears stung my eyes, but I refused to let them fall. "Maybe he doesn't know me now. But I know him, Mom. And I believe, with everything in me, that the universe doesn't bring people into your life—whether through words or chance—without a reason."

Her expression softened for a moment, but then she turned away, frustration taking over again. "You're throwing your life away for a dream. Do you understand that? You're engaged, for God's sake! You can't keep living in this fantasy. One day, you'll wake up and realise it was all for nothing."

I took a deep breath, steadying myself. "I'd rather live in this dream, where I feel alive than settle for a reality where my soul is suffocating."

She sighed, defeated. "You're impossible. I can't talk to you when you're like this." She picked up her purse and headed toward the door, pausing only briefly. "I hope you wake up soon, Seraphine. Before it's too late."

The door closed behind her, and I stood in silence, her words lingering in the air like smoke.

And in that moment, I knew one thing for certain: I had found my poet, even if no one else understood it. And I didn't care if our lines never intersected. All I knew was that my soul belonged to him.

Another year drifted by like a slow-moving tide, carrying with it the weight of indecision and compromise. Days blurred into nights, and the weeks folded themselves neatly into months, each one looking eerily like the last.

It's strange how time moves when you're not living the life you want. Every day feels endless, yet the year disappears in the blink of an eye. I kept telling myself, next month, next week, tomorrow, but the courage never came.

I had been cracking for years now. A little piece of myself fell away every time I said yes when I wanted to say no, every time I let someone else's idea of my life take precedence over my own.

And my family? They meant well. I knew they did. My mother's sharp words echoed in my mind, but they were rooted in love, in fear that I'd throw away everything safe for something uncertain. But didn't she see? Didn't anyone see that I was already throwing something away—myself?

Alasdair felt like the only truth I'd ever known. I held his books like lifelines, and read his words like they were meant just for me. And maybe that was foolish. Maybe my mother was right, and I was confusing fantasy with reality. But if that wasn't real, why did it feel more honest than anything else in my life?

I spent my nights tracing sentences, running my fingers over his name on the cover, wondering if he knew I existed. Wondering if the universe was laughing at me, dangling this impossible dream just out of reach.

And yet, I didn't do anything. I was frozen between the life I had and the life I wanted, too scared to leap, too scared to stay. I wasted another year waiting for the right moment, but deep down, I knew that the moment wouldn't come unless I made it.

I looked in the mirror and barely recognised the girl staring back. She was tired, worn down by a love she couldn't have and a life she didn't want.

How many more years would I let pass before I stop waiting and start living? The fear of staying the same was starting to outweigh the fear of change, and I wondered if that was what it took to finally leap.

## 13
# Alasdair

After four years of knowing her—not through conversations or shared moments, but through her words and the emotions she bled onto every page—I finally decided it was time to see her in person. Time to step beyond the world of imagination and meet my poem.

The flight across the country felt surreal, the hum of the plane fading into the background as I clutched my worn copy of To Be a Poem. My thumb brushed over her name on the cover. The name itself felt like a poem.

When I arrived, the city's unfamiliar energy buzzed around me, but I couldn't focus on anything except the bookstore, my only destination. I reached the venue hours early, only to find a line already wrapping around the block. Fans chatted excitedly, their voices rising in admiration for the person I had come to love.

Finally, the line moved, slow and steady, each step bringing me closer to her. Through the glass storefront, I caught my first glimpse of her. My breath caught.

She sat at a small table surrounded by stacks of her books, her presence both radiant and grounded. Her red hair gleamed under the soft lights like a flame, falling in waves over her shoulders. But it was her eyes—vivid green, like spring breaking through a winter forest—that stopped me cold.

When it was my turn, after hours of standing, I approached her, my heartbeat loud in my ears. She looked up, and for a moment, time slowed. Her green eyes met mine, and I forgot how to breathe. It was as though every line of her poetry had leapt off the page and come alive in her gaze.

"Hi," she said, her voice soft and melodic, like the verses she wrote.

I stared, unable to form words. She tilted her head slightly, a small, curious smile playing on her lips. Finally, I found my voice.

"Hi," I managed to whisper, my throat dry.

"Who should I make this out to?" she asked, her pen poised over the title page of my book.

I wanted to say my name—Alasdair—but the syllables seemed stuck in my throat. I stood there, frozen, my heart pounding in my chest. She waited for a moment, her gaze never leaving mine.

"It's okay," she said gently, her lips curving into a small smile. "Take your time."

Her kindness only made it harder to speak. My name felt insignificant in her presence, like it didn't deserve to be spoken aloud.

After all, how could I, an ordinary person, possibly belong in her world of poetry and brilliance?

Finally, I managed to hold out the book to her, my hand trembling slightly. She hesitated for a moment, then smiled again.

"All right," she said softly. She opened the book and began to write, her pen gliding gracefully over the page.

When she handed it back to me, her green eyes searched mine. "I hope you enjoy it," she said, her voice warm.

"Your book was a window I didn't know I needed, and through it, I saw pieces of myself I'd forgotten existed."

I said, my voice trembling, as if the words themselves held the weight of everything I had been carrying. I looked at her, unsure if she could truly understand the depth of what I meant. It wasn't just a compliment; it was a confession, a release of all the emotions her words had stirred within me.

She paused, her eyes softening as she took in my words. There was a quiet moment between us, a space filled with unspoken understanding.

"I didn't expect it to touch you like that. After all, it's just a book." She murmured, her voice barely audible, but there was a tremor in it—a vulnerability I hadn't seen before.

"It was never just a book. It was a confession, a map, a doorway to something I didn't dare hope for—you."

The words left my lips like they had been waiting for years to be spoken. As I said them, I saw her eyes widen, as if she hadn't expected the depth of what I was saying. For a moment, time slowed down. It was just us, being there in the chaos of the crowd, an invisible thread connecting our souls.

And then, from behind me, I heard a sharp voice, "Please move, your time is up." The impatience in the person's voice echoed through the air, and I felt a shove at my back. My feet stumbled slightly, but my eyes never left hers.

The person behind me pushed again, harder this time, frustration in their tone growing louder. I tried to steady myself, but all I could focus on was the way she was looking at me—her gaze intense, searching, like she was trying to understand the gravity of my words.

In that brief, fleeting moment, I couldn't bring myself to look away, even as I was pushed further to the side. I felt the distance between us grow, but it didn't matter. Our eyes locked in silent understanding, a promise that even if the world was trying to pull us apart, what we had just shared could never be erased.

The person called her name, and just like that, the world shifted. She blinked, breaking the connection between us. The magic that had felt so tangible a second ago seemed to evaporate, replaced by the reality of the line, the noise, the crowd. She turned toward the person who had called her, her expression momentarily clouded by the shift in attention.

For a moment, I stood there, frozen, as if waiting for time to rewind so I could hold onto those few seconds longer. But it was gone, like a dream fading in the morning light. The world rushed back into focus, but I couldn't shake the feeling that something important had just happened—that something unspoken had passed between us.

I took a step forward, but the crowd surged, and just like that, she was lost to it. I stood there, her presence still lingering, unsure of what had just transpired, but knowing that whatever it was, it was something I couldn't just forget.

As I exited the store, the weight of the moment began to settle, a strange mixture of peace and longing. I didn't know what the future held. I didn't know if our paths would cross again or if she would even remember me. But I couldn't deny the truth of what I'd felt in that brief exchange.

Some connections weren't meant to be understood immediately. Maybe I wasn't meant to know what it all meant yet. But as I walked away from the bookstore, my heart still racing, I knew one thing for sure: I had seen her. Really seen her. She had seen me, too. And that our eyes had finally met.

I walked down the street, the sounds of the city humming in the background, but it all felt distant, muffled. The crowd had swallowed me up, and yet, I felt more alone than ever. My mind replayed the encounter over and over again, each moment more vivid than the last. The feel of her eyes on me, the weight of her words, and the way the world had seemed to stop for just a second—it all lingered.

I reached a small park and sat on a bench, trying to process the whirlwind of emotions. I opened the book she had signed, running my fingers over the ink of her handwriting, the familiar loop of her signature grounding me somehow. I could still feel the faint warmth of her hand where the book had passed from hers to mine, as if the connection hadn't entirely faded, even though the moment was gone.

What had that look meant? What was it that had passed between us, even as the world had continued to push us apart? Was it just a fleeting spark, or was it something more—something that had been building for years, all through the words she had written, through the pages of the book I had carried with me everywhere?

I glanced at the signature again, her name written carefully in the corner of the page: Seraphine Mitchell. It felt like an echo, like something waiting to come alive. Maybe I wasn't supposed to understand it all at that moment. Maybe there was something deeper to be discovered, something that time would reveal.

But right now, I had to face the truth: I was still here. Alone, but not entirely. Her words had lived in me, had shaped me. And today, despite the briefness of our meeting, I could feel the impact of her presence within me. It wasn't just about meeting the person behind the words. It was about what those words had done to me—how they had reshaped the way I saw the world and myself.

The city was sprawling and unfamiliar, but I felt grounded in this moment, in this realisation. For the first time in a long while, I didn't feel like I was waiting for something to happen. The moment had already happened. It had been brief, yes, but it was enough to stir something in me that I couldn't ignore.

As the sun began to set, casting a golden light over the park, I closed the book and tucked it into my bag. The world was moving around me, full of voices and faces I would never know, but I had seen something today. Something real. Something beyond words.

I didn't know what would happen next, but I knew one thing for sure: I couldn't go back to who I was before I met her—before the words and the silence between us spoke louder than anything I had ever known.

The flight back home was almost haunting. Now that I had seen her, I just couldn't unsee her. Her appearance kept coming to my mind, a series of vivid images that danced in my thoughts like an unfinished poem. Her red hair, like flames caught in the light, her green eyes, full of stories and secrets, the way she'd smiled at me—

soft, understanding, almost as if she knew exactly who I was before I even spoke. Every detail replayed in my head, not like a memory, but like a living, breathing thing, constantly shifting and evolving.

## 14
# Seraphine

It was a long day. My hand was worn off by giving autographs. Each signature felt more like a gesture than a personal connection. The crowd had been relentless, eager to meet the face behind the words they had poured over, but the exhaustion was settling in. Every smile I forced felt heavier than the last, and the weight of being "on" for hours drained me, leaving my shoulders tight and my thoughts scattered.

But even as the physical exhaustion took hold, my mind kept circling back to him. The man who had stood in line, his eyes locking onto mine with an intensity that felt almost too familiar, too deep for a simple exchange at a book signing. There was something in the way he spoke, the rawness in his words, I could still hear it in my mind, the way he said it—like it wasn't just a compliment, but a confession, a lifeline.

I shook my head, trying to clear the lingering thoughts. But it was hard. His eyes—those dark eyes, filled with something I couldn't understand—kept invading my space. The way he had looked at me, not as a writer but as a person. It was unsettling in a way, as if everything I had created, every word, every line, had led me to this one moment.

"I'll never see him again," I told myself. "It was just a moment. A fleeting connection." But deep down, I couldn't help the part of me that wished I could somehow find him again.

When I got home, I collapsed onto the couch, too tired to do anything but stare blankly at the walls. The book—Before Our Eyes Met—was still sitting on the coffee table, its cover staring up at me, as if waiting for me to open it. But I was too drained, mentally and physically, to even pick it up. The event had worn me thin, leaving me with little energy for anything else. I made a mental note to read it the next day.

The next morning, the world felt quiet, like a calm after the storm. I woke up early, a habit I'd developed to make space for the things that mattered. As I reached for the book, I felt a curious tension in my chest, an excitement that had been missing for a while.

Reading his books was nothing new, but the feeling I got each time felt so new.

*That's how I have known you, before our eyes met. Through your words, through the ink you bled onto the page, I had already found a piece of you. I didn't need to meet you to understand your thoughts, your emotions, your struggles. Your words had painted a picture in my mind, a portrait of someone I didn't even know yet but had already started to fall for.*

*It was strange, knowing someone so intimately without ever having spoken to them, without even knowing their voice. Yet somehow, your writing filled the spaces I didn't even know I had.*

*Before our eyes met, I was already drawn to you—by the beauty of your mind, the rawness of your vulnerability. Your words had already taken root in me. It was no longer just the words I had fallen in love with; it was you. And if someday our eyes finally do meet, I hope our love still stays as pure as it is now.*

It felt like a love confession. He seemed so close and yet so far. The distance between us was only real if I closed the book, if I stopped reading. And I was not ready for 'The End.' Maybe the ink on our pages was invisible to others, but not to us. We saw the truth—lines we were always meant to cross.

I opened my laptop and started writing my reply. Months and years passed, and I found myself writing to my unknown lover, while still engaged to someone else. But the truth was, I wasn't in love with Asher. I had never truly been in love with him—not in the way a partner should be. I stayed with him because he was familiar, because he fit the mould of what was expected, of what was easy. But all along, I knew something was missing. What I hadn't realised, though, was that Asher wasn't the only one who was drifting away.

Alasdair, on the other hand, felt different—unlike anyone I had ever known, even from afar. Loving him didn't feel like a choice; it was as natural as breathing, as inevitable as the turning of the seasons. I loved him in the way the tide loves the shore, always drawn back no matter how far it strayed. It wasn't the kind of love that demanded attention or validation—it simply was, steady and unwavering.

With Alasdair, it was as though I had found a missing piece of myself, one I hadn't known was lost. I didn't just love him for who he was, but for the way he saw the world, for the way his words seemed to reach into the most hidden parts of my soul and bring them into the light. Loving him felt like coming home, even though we had never shared a space, never exchanged more than a few fleeting words. It was love in its purest form—untouched by circumstance, untainted by expectation.

And yet, it was a love that existed in the in-between, caught in the pages of a book, in the unspoken spaces between us. It was beautiful, and it was maddening, but above all, it was real. Falling in love with him wasn't loud. It was quiet, like a leaf drifting to the ground—a feeling that grew with every page I turned.

## 15
# Alasdair

Six years of conversing through books had unraveled me in ways I never thought possible. I had fallen deeply, irrevocably, in love—not with a face or a voice, but with a soul I had come to know through the pages of someone else's words. Seraphine was more than just a name on a cover to me; she was the keeper of my secrets, the translator of emotions I hadn't yet found the courage to speak. With every sentence she wrote, it felt as though she was stitching pieces of my fractured heart back together.

Each of her books had been a revelation. They were more than just stories; they were conversations, tender and intimate, where the spaces between the words seemed to hum with meaning only I could understand. With every new release, I would wait with bated breath, devouring her sentences as though they held the answers to questions I hadn't yet asked. And when I wrote my own stories, it was her I was speaking to, even if she didn't know it.

Through metaphors and prose, I confessed my longing, my admiration, my love. I poured my soul into every chapter, imagining her reading my words and feeling the same quiet, undeniable connection I felt when I read hers. Yet as the years passed, I grew restless. The distance between us, the anonymity of it all, began to weigh heavily on my heart.

I wanted more. I wanted her to see me—the one who had fallen in love with her through the spaces between the lines. I wanted her to know me the way I felt I knew her.

So, in my last book, I decided to take a leap of faith. For six years, I had hidden behind layers of poetry and carefully crafted sentences, too afraid to reveal the depths of my feelings. But this time, I stripped it all back and wrote the truth in the simplest words I could muster:

"I wish you could see me, just like you saw my soul."

It wasn't just a line in the book—it was a plea, a confession, a hope. I published the book and released it into the world, knowing it would eventually find its way to her. I imagined her holding it, reading those words, and feeling the same spark that had ignited in me so many years ago.

And then, I waited. At first, the waiting was filled with anticipation. Each passing day brought with it a flutter of excitement, a whisper of possibility. I told myself to be patient, that she needed time to process what I had written, to craft her response. But as the days turned into weeks and the weeks into months, my hope began to falter.

A year passed, and still, there was no reply. Just silence. I told myself she was busy, that life had simply gotten in the way. But as the second year came and went, the silence became unbearable.

I replayed every moment in my mind, wondering if I had been too bold, if my words had scared her away. Doubts began to creep in like shadows, whispering questions I didn't want to answer. Had she read it? Had she understood what I meant? Or worse, had she understood and chosen not to respond?

I tried to move on, to focus on my work, but the emptiness lingered. My writing felt hollow, my words lifeless. I would sit at my desk for hours, staring at blank pages, unable to summon the inspiration that had once come so easily. Even reading her old books brought little comfort. They still moved me, still stirred something deep within me, but they were tinged with the ache of unfulfilled longing.

I kept telling myself to let go, to accept that whatever connection I thought we had was one-sided. But my heart refused to listen.

As the second year without a reply came to an end, I found myself asking the same question over and over: Had it all been in my head?

The uncertainty was the hardest part. It gnawed at me, filling the silence with doubt. And yet, beneath the doubt, a small ember of hope remained, stubborn and unyielding.

Because even if she never replied, even if she never saw me the way I saw her, I couldn't regret the love I had felt. It had shaped me, inspired me, given me something to hold onto when the world felt too heavy. And for that, I would always be grateful.

But being in love, I couldn't keep it all within myself anymore. It hurt in a way that words couldn't touch, the kind of ache that settles deep into your chest and refuses to let go. So, I did the only thing I could think of—I called Albert, the friend who had unknowingly set all of this into motion.

"Albert, I need to talk," I said, my voice low and strained.

"What now?" he replied, his tone halfway between annoyance and concern. "You sound like you've been through a war."

"It's about her," I said, hesitating for just a moment before spilling everything—the years of writing back and forth through books, the connection I felt every time I read her words, the bold confession I had finally worked up the courage to put in my last book, and the deafening silence that had followed.

There was a pause on the other end of the line before Albert sighed. "What?" he said finally, his voice sharp with disbelief. "I thought you were over it. I thought it was just a fanboy moment, Alasdair. I didn't know it'd actually make you—"

"Crazy?" I finished for him, bitterness creeping into my voice.

"Look, I didn't mean it like that," he said quickly, though his tone didn't soften. "I just— I thought it was a phase. If I'd known, I would've never given you that book. I gave it to you because I thought it was a good read, not because I wanted you to fall in love with someone you can never have."

His words stung, but I pushed past the sharpness in my chest. "You don't understand," I said. "It's not just about her being an author or her being famous. It's about everything she's written. It's about the way her words spoke to me like no one else ever has. It's like she reached inside me and found things I didn't even know I felt. How can that be nothing?"

Albert exhaled, his frustration barely contained. "Alasdair, she's a writer. That's what they do. They write things that feel personal because that's their job. You're not the only one who feels this way.

I'm sure there are thousands of people out there who think she's writing just for them."

"But what about all those words? The ones that felt so specific, so real? It can't be that they meant nothing, right?"

Albert was silent for a moment, and for a brief second, I thought he might understand. But then he spoke, and his voice was cold, practical, and distant. "Alasdair, she's a famous author. How can you live in this delusion that she's writing for you? It could be about anybody. Hell, it could be about no one. It's fiction."

I opened my mouth to protest, but he cut me off before I could speak. "And don't you have social media?" he snapped. "This is exactly why I tell you to join the modern world. Go check her social media. Look her up. You'll find the answer you're looking for."

The line went dead before I could reply. I sat there, staring at my phone, his words ringing in my ears. I hated the idea of searching her online—something about it felt invasive, wrong, like I was prying into a part of her life that wasn't meant for me. But the desperation in my chest outweighed my hesitations. If there was even the smallest chance of finding a clue, I had to try.

Reluctantly, I downloaded the app, my fingers clumsy as I set up an account. It felt foreign, awkward, like stepping into a world I didn't belong in. But as soon as I typed her name into the search bar and her profile appeared, my heart sank.

There it was, staring back at me in black and white: "Retired Author."

I read it again, and then again, hoping it would change somehow, that I had misread the words or misunderstood their meaning. But no matter how many times I blinked, they stayed the same.

Retired.

The word hit me like a punch to the stomach. Retired meant she was done. It meant no more books, no more words, no more conversations between us. It meant that whatever connection I thought we had—real or imagined—was over.

I closed the app, unable to look at her profile any longer. The phone slipped from my hand onto the couch beside me, and I leaned forward, burying my face in my hands.

Albert was right. I had been living in a delusion, chasing a love that was never mine to begin with. But knowing that didn't make it hurt any less. If anything, it only made the ache worse.

## 16

# Alasdair

Life had become a blur, a series of empty routines I drifted through while my heart clung desperately to fragments of her words. All I did was keep going back to her books, poring over sentences that felt like they were carved out of my own soul, meant only for me.

*If our words can find each other, maybe we can, too.*

She had written. A hopeful promise, a lifeline I had held onto for years. But if that were true, where was she now? Why did she leave everything behind—leave me behind?

*I don't know your face, but I know your soul. And I'd trade every word I've written just to meet you between the lines.*

That line haunted me the most. I remembered the first time I read it, how it felt like she had cracked me open and seen everything I was too afraid to show the world. Did it mean nothing? Was it just a clever turn of phrase meant for anyone who read it, or had it been a whisper meant for me?

The questions tore at me in the silence of my small apartment, where her books sat stacked beside my bed, dog-eared and worn from years of rereading. Every time I opened them, I found something new, another line that felt like it carried a piece of her heart—and mine.

*Your sentences have become my favourite place to hide, because, within them, I feel seen.*

Seen. That word was everything. For so long, her words had been my refuge, the place I turned to when the world felt too loud, too overwhelming. I had believed, foolishly perhaps, that I wasn't alone in that feeling. But now, it seemed she had hidden elsewhere, leaving me to search for her in the empty spaces she had left behind.

I tried to convince myself it was all in my head, that I had read too much into her words. But how could I not? They were too personal, too raw, too alive to be mere fiction. It was as if she had reached out through the pages, grasping for something or someone.

I flipped through her books again, landing on another line I had underlined years ago:

*What would you do if you found me? Would you run, or would you stay and let us unravel together?*

I had always thought my answer would be obvious. I would stay. I would let every barrier fall, let myself be unraveled by her, for her. But now, with her gone, with no sign of her return, I wondered if she had already run.

The pain of it was sharp, a deep ache that refused to dull. It wasn't just that I missed her words—it was that I missed the hope they had given me. The hope that maybe two strangers could find each other between the lines.

*I've never seen you smile, never heard your laugh, but your words made me love them anyway.*

It was a line I'd read a thousand times, one that had burned itself into my memory like an unanswered question. I couldn't shake how deeply it resonated, how it felt like it had been written for me, and only me.

Every time I revisited those words, they struck a chord I couldn't name. I'd lie awake at night, replaying that single sentence in my mind, wondering if it was possible for someone so far away, so untouchable, to have glimpsed even a shadow of me in their words.

How could a line meant for anyone feel like it belonged only to me?

All I did was walk. From the gas station to the grocery store at the end of the street, I traced the same path day after day. I bought no gas, no groceries. I didn't need them. What I needed was something I couldn't find on a shelf. So, I kept walking.

I walked along the children's park, where laughter rang out like a distant echo of something I used to know. I passed in front of the city prison, its walls tall and unyielding, a reminder that some things are out of reach no matter how much you long for them. Sometimes I wandered into the old age homes, sitting quietly as I asked the wise men and women for advice. They looked at me with eyes that held too much pity, like I was a lost child at a book fair, clutching a list of titles I'd never find.

Other times, I went to the orphanage. The children there didn't bother with pity; they laughed instead, their bright, unfiltered honesty cutting deeper than the softest sighs of the elderly. They told me I was a stupid adult, wasting my time chasing something invisible. Their laughter echoed as I left, but I couldn't bring myself to be angry. Maybe they were right.

And so, with all the pity and laughter trailing behind me like a second shadow, I kept walking.

I walked up and down the stairs of my old apartment building, clutching her first book in my hand like it was the only thing tethering me to the world. The pages had grown soft with wear, the edges curling as though they'd absorbed my restlessness. I sat at the top of the stairs sometimes, reading and rereading the same passages until the words lost meaning. Then I went back down, my feet heavy, my heart heavier.

I went to cafés, the kind with mismatched chairs and baristas who don't smile much. I sat in the corner without ordering anything, her book open on the table before me. I pretended to read, but mostly I just stared out the window, watching people come and go, wondering if she ever walked past this very spot.

Sometimes, the staff asked me to leave. "We need the table," they said, or "This isn't a library." I apologised and stepped outside, but I always came back. I returned the next day or the day after that, always to the same corner, as if something magical might happen if I waited long enough.

The city became my labyrinth, and I walked its streets like a restless ghost, searching for something I couldn't name. Fragments from her books lodged themselves in the untouched corners of my soul.

*If you keep moving, you'll find it. Whatever 'it' is.*

That line. I held onto it like a mantra, even though I didn't know what "it" was anymore. Was it her? Was it the feeling she gave me? Or was it the piece of myself I lost when she disappeared?

The truth was, I didn't know why I walked. But I did. Every step felt like a question, every path like a plea. "Will today be the day I find what I'm looking for? Or will I keep circling the same streets, wearing down the soles of my shoes and the edges of my hope?"

I walked past the places I knew she wrote about, the landmarks she described with such vivid detail. I imagined her there, sitting on a park bench or leaning against the railing of a bridge, her notebook open in her lap. I pictured her pen moving swiftly, her brow furrowed in concentration, and I wondered if she ever thought someone would read those words and fall in love—not just with the stories, but with her.

And so I kept walking. It was the only way I could keep her close, even if she was gone, even if she never knew I was walking toward her all along.

## 17
## Alasdair

Albert came to my house one afternoon with a suitcase in hand, an unspoken determination spread across his face. He didn't ask for permission, didn't wait for an invitation—he just stepped in and declared, "I'm staying. You can't keep living like this."

I didn't argue. I didn't have the energy.

For the first few days, he busied himself with the little things: cleaning up the apartment, throwing away the uneaten food that had been rotting in the fridge, opening the curtains to let in the light I hadn't realised I'd been avoiding. He tried to talk to me, but my answers were short, my voice hollow.

"You need to go to therapy, Alasdair," he said one evening, his voice firm but not unkind. "This isn't just heartbreak. This is delusion."

I didn't respond. I was lying on the couch, staring at the ceiling, her words playing over and over in my head like a broken record. "If our words can find each other, maybe we can, too."

"You're not even listening to me, are you?" Albert sighed, his frustration barely contained. "You think this is normal? Throwing up blood? Stopping eating? Walking around places where you don't belong?"

I flinched at his words but still didn't answer.

Albert didn't let up. He grabbed the trash can from the corner of the room and dumped its contents onto the coffee table. Empty wrappers, crumpled tissues, and the remnants of stale crackers I'd barely nibbled on. "Look at this! This isn't living, Alasdair. This is you letting yourself waste away over someone who doesn't even know you exist!"

That stung, and he knew it.

"You don't understand," I finally said, my voice a rasp.

"Then make me understand!" Albert shouted, and for the first time in years, I saw tears glistening in his eyes. "Tell me how you think this ends. Tell me what you think is going to happen when you sit here starving yourself, clinging to words that weren't written for you."

I sat up slowly, my head heavy, my body weak. "She does know me," I said. "Not by name, not by face, but by soul. Her words… they weren't just written. They were meant. For me."

Albert let out a bitter laugh and sank into the armchair across from me, rubbing his temples. "Do you hear yourself? Do you even realise how far gone you sound?" He looked at me, his eyes filled with a mix of anger and worry. "Alasdair, please. I'm begging you. Go to therapy. Talk to someone who can actually help you. Because I can't keep watching you kill yourself like this."

The room fell silent except for the faint sound of the refrigerator in the kitchen. I wanted to tell him he was wrong, that I was fine, that I didn't need therapy. But I couldn't. The truth was, I knew he was right.

"I'll think about it," I mumbled.

Albert shook his head, standing up and walking toward the kitchen. "Thinking isn't enough, Alasdair. Thinking won't save you. Action will."

A few minutes later, he returned with a plate of food—toast and eggs, simple but warm. He set it on the table in front of me. "Eat," he said.

"I'm not hungry."

"Eat anyway. Do you think throwing up blood is normal? You think this is fine? If you won't do it for yourself, do it for me. Because I can't sit here and watch you destroy yourself."

His voice cracked on the last word, and I saw just how much my pain was affecting him. I picked up the toast hesitantly, my hands trembling, and took a small bite. It tasted like cardboard, but Albert's eyes didn't leave me until I finished the entire plate.

"That's a start," he said softly, taking the plate and heading back to the kitchen. "And go to the doctor, will you?" he shouted from the kitchen.

"I'll see."

The next few months passed quickly, a strange mix of progress and emptiness. At Albert's insistence, I went to the therapist.

My therapist, a gentle but unyielding woman named Dr. Collins, asked questions that I didn't want to answer. "Why do you think you've tied so much of your identity to this person you've never met?" she asked one afternoon, her pen poised over her notepad.

I looked away, staring at the sunlight streaming through her office window. "Because she's the only one who's ever understood me," I said finally.

Dr. Collins nodded thoughtfully. "And what does it mean to be understood? Is it possible you're projecting your own desires onto her words?"

Her question hung in the air like a challenge, but I couldn't bring myself to respond.

Each session chipped away at the walls I'd built around myself, but the process was draining. I went home feeling exposed, as if the therapy was unraveling me instead of putting me back together.

Albert, ever the loyal friend, refused to let me retreat into my old habits. He cooked meals and sat across from me at the table, watching with determination as I forced myself to eat. He accompanied me on walks, steering me away from the orphanages and old age homes I used to haunt, and insisted we try new routes.

"It's time to make new memories," he said one afternoon as we strolled through a park on the other side of town.

But no matter how hard I tried, nothing seemed more draining than losing touch with Seraphine. Her absence was a constant ache, a shadow that followed me everywhere.

I reread her books obsessively, searching for some hidden clue I might have missed, some indication of where she had gone or why she had disappeared. Her words still felt like lifelines, but they also felt like ghosts, haunting me with the possibility of what could have been.

*If our words can find each other, maybe we can, too.*

That line used to fill me with hope. Now, it felt like a cruel joke. If it were true, why had she vanished? Why had she retired without a word? Why had she left me—left us—behind?

"She's just a writer," Albert reminded me whenever I voiced my frustrations aloud. "You're projecting a relationship onto someone who never even knew you existed."

But I couldn't accept that. It wasn't just her books—it was the connection I felt, the unspoken bond between her words and my soul. It wasn't a delusion. It couldn't be.

Yet, as the months passed, I began to wonder if I was fooling myself. Therapy helped me unpack my feelings, to recognise the ways I had built my identity around her words, but it didn't make the ache go away.

I missed her. Not just her books, but her. The version of her I had come to know through her writing, the woman who had bared her soul in metaphors and prose.

One day, as I sat on the edge of my bed, holding her last book in my hands, I whispered into the silence, "Why did you leave?"

The book offered no answers, just the same sentences I had read a hundred times before. But this time, they didn't feel like lifelines. They felt like farewells.

I even went to a doctor and got to know things that I wished I better not knew. At that point, I didn't want anything romantic with her, just contact, just answers would've been enough for me. Answers to not questions asking why she left me, but answers to questions asking if she was alright.

## 18
## Alasdair

The air outside was crisp, colder than it should have been for late spring. I hadn't planned on leaving the house that day, but something about the way Albert looked at me during breakfast—half hopeful, half exasperated—pushed me out the door.

"Take a walk," he had said. "A real one this time. No wandering aimlessly, no sitting in front of bookstores waiting for her next release. Just…walk."

And so, I walked. Not to the park or the grocery store or the orphanage, but to somewhere unfamiliar, somewhere I hadn't let my thoughts dwell.

The library.

It wasn't the first place that came to mind when I thought of starting fresh, but it seemed fitting. Seraphine loved books, and somewhere deep down, I hoped that stepping into a library might feel like stepping into her world.

The smell hit me first—that familiar blend of aged paper and something faintly woody. It was comforting in a way I hadn't expected. Rows upon rows of shelves towered above me, each one crammed with stories waiting to be told. For the first time in months, I felt a flicker of curiosity.

I wandered the aisles without purpose, letting my fingers graze the spines of books at random. I wasn't looking for anything in particular, but then my eyes caught a familiar title tucked away in the corner of the fiction section.

It wasn't one of Seraphine's books—it was one of mine.

I pulled it off the shelf, staring at the cover as though it might hold answers to questions I hadn't thought to ask. It felt strange, seeing it here, sandwiched between other authors who probably had no idea their work was sitting next to mine.

And then I saw it—slipped between the pages was a piece of paper, folded neatly in half. My heart skipped. Slowly, I opened it.

The note was handwritten, the ink slightly smudged, but the words were unmistakable.

*"I've read this book so many times, I could recite it from memory. Thank you for writing something that feels like coming home. I wish I could tell you how much it means to me, but for now, this will have to do. Maybe one day, I'll get the chance to thank you in person."*

There was no signature, but I didn't need one. I knew who had written it. I knew the handwriting.

My hands trembled as I refolded the note and slipped it back into the book. For a moment, I just stood there, trying to steady my breathing.

She had been here. At some point, Seraphine had held this book, had written those words, had left them here for someone to find. For me to find.

I clutched the book to my chest and turned toward the librarian's desk.

"Excuse me," I said, my voice unsteady. "This book—do you know when it was last checked out?"

The librarian, an older woman with a kind face, glanced at the barcode and tapped a few keys on her computer.

"It hasn't been checked out in years," she said. "But it's been read a lot here in the library. People leave it on the tables all the time."

"Does anyone come here often to read it?" I pressed, my pulse quickening.

She hesitated, her brow furrowing in thought. "There was a woman, maybe a year or two ago. She'd sit in the corner by the window and read for hours. I remember because she always brought a red notebook with her. She seemed thoughtful."

My heart felt like it was about to burst. "Do you remember anything else about her? Anything at all?"

The librarian shook her head apologetically. "I'm sorry, dear. She stopped coming after a while."

Frustration threatened to overwhelm me, but I clung to the tiny thread of hope. She had been here. She had left me a message, however small, however cryptic.

It wasn't much, but it was something.

As I left the library, the book clutched tightly in my hands, I made a decision.

I would find her.

Not as the fan who had once idolised her, not as the broken man who had clung to her words like a lifeline, but as someone ready to meet her between the lines.

For the first time in years, I felt alive.

The coffee shop was dimly lit, its warm amber glow spilling onto the cobblestone street outside. It was nearly empty, save for a barista lazily cleaning the counter and a man in the corner, tapping away at his laptop. The faint hum of jazz drifted through the air, mingling with the sharp scent of freshly brewed espresso.

I hadn't planned on coming here. My feet had carried me without thought, still buzzing from the encounter at the library. The book was tucked under my arm, its weight both comforting and electrifying.

I settled at a corner table near the window. It overlooked the street, where the occasional passerby hurried by, their coats pulled tight against the chilly late afternoon air.

I was just about to get up and order my coffee when my eyes fell on something bright.

A flash of red.

## 19
## Alasdair

It wasn't unusual to see someone with red hair, but this wasn't just any shade. It was her shade—the unmistakable copper-red that I had imagined a thousand times. It caught the light as she moved, spilling over her shoulders like fire.

I froze.

She was sitting at a table on the far side of the room, half-turned away from me, her head bent low over a red notebook. One of her hands was on her forehead, making her look distressed.

The same notebook the librarian had mentioned.

My fingers gripped the edge of the table as I stared, trying to steady the storm inside me. Could it really be her? Was this another coincidence, another cruel trick of fate, or had I finally found her?

I debated for what felt like an eternity. Should I go to her? Should I wait? What if it wasn't her? What if it was, and she didn't want to see me?

But then she did something that made my heart stop.

She lifted her pen, hesitated for a moment, and then scribbled something onto the page. As she did, she turned just enough for me to catch a glimpse of her profile.

It was her.

Seraphine.

The woman I had spent years searching for was sitting just a few tables away, unaware of my existence.

I stood, my chair scraping against the floor. The sound was loud, cutting through the quiet hum of the café, and for a split second, her head tilted in my direction.

I froze, but she didn't look up. Her focus returned to the notebook, her pen gliding across the page.

Every step I took toward her felt heavier than the last, my pulse pounding in my ears. When I finally reached her table, I hesitated, biting my lower lip in anxiousness. As I neared her, I saw that she was wearing an apron. An apron that had the coffee shop's name written on it.

Slowly, she looked up, her eyes meeting mine for the first time.

They were exactly as I had seen years ago—deep, soulful, and impossibly familiar, as though I had known them my entire life.

She immediately stood up, straightening her fit, and asked, "How can I help you, sir?"

"You work here?" I asked.

"Yes. I was just taking a break since there were no new customers. What can I get for you?"

She didn't recognise me. Of course. How could she? After all, I was just one of those fans she meets every day.

"Coffee. Two cups please." I said, my eyes not leaving hers. She bit her lips a little in nervousness and nodded. While leaving, she released a deep sigh, as if she was just taken out of her stressful thoughts.

I slid into the seat beside hers. Our books were tucked inside my coat, the edges of their worn pages pressing against my chest. If she didn't recognise me already, I had no intention of making it easier for her. Not yet.

I wanted to know the truth. And truth, I had learned, flows more freely to strangers than to familiar faces.

She returned moments later, two cups of coffee balanced carefully in her hands. She placed them on the table with grace, her fingers brushing the surface of the cup as if testing its warmth.

"Sit down," I said, gesturing to the chair beside me.

Her brow furrowed slightly, surprised. "Pardon?"

"This one's for me," I said, reaching for one of the cups and cradling it in my hands. "And this one, for you. Have a seat. You look tired."

She hesitated, her eyes flickering between me and the coffee. For a moment, I thought she might refuse. But then, a small, polite smile curved her lips, and she sat down across from me.

"You really didn't have to," she said softly, her voice polite but distant.

"And yet, here we are," I replied, meeting her gaze. "Consider it a gift from one stranger to another."

Her smile lingered, but there was something guarded in her expression, as though she were carefully choosing how much of herself to reveal. She wrapped her hands around the cup, her fingers delicate against the porcelain.

"You must be new around here," she said, breaking the silence. "I don't usually see people... well, offering strangers coffee."

"I suppose I'm not from around here," I said, shrugging. "But I couldn't just watch you walking back and forth with that tired look on your face. Sometimes, a little coffee and company make all the difference."

Her smile faltered for a moment, and I wondered if my words had struck a nerve. She looked down at the coffee, stirring it absentmindedly with a small spoon.

"I guess I do look a little worn out," she admitted, almost to herself. "It's been a long few years."

I leaned back slightly, keeping my tone light. "The world has a way of doing that to people."

She nodded, her eyes distant, as though she were seeing something far beyond the café walls. Then, as if snapping out of a memory, she looked back at me.

"So, what brings you here?" she asked, her voice laced with polite curiosity.

I paused, considering my answer. "I suppose I'm just passing through," I said carefully. "Looking for answers in a world full of questions."

"Well," she said quietly, "if you find any, let me know. I could use a few myself."

I took a sip of my coffee, the warmth spreading through me as I studied her face. The walls she had so carefully built seemed to crack ever so slightly, and I knew this was my chance to get closer to the truth.

"And what about you?" I asked, keeping my tone gentle. "What's a writer like you doing in a place like this, far from the pages where she belongs?"

Her head snapped up, her eyes narrowing slightly. For a second, I thought I'd pushed too far. But then she tilted her head, curiosity dancing in her gaze.

"How do you know I'm a writer?" she asked, a faint challenge in her voice.

"Oh! Just my assumption." I stuttered. "I saw you scribbling something on that notebook. So I thought you must be a writer or something similar."

She stared at me for a moment, and I could feel her mind working, trying to piece together who I was. But I kept my expression neutral, my tone steady, as if I were just another stranger sharing a table and a cup of coffee.

"Well, you made a right guess. But I'm not one anymore. I've retired." She said, taking a sip of her coffee.

"Once a writer, always a writer." I said with a mischievous smile, raising one of my brows. She laughed, and I swear to god that it was the most beautiful thing I had ever seen.

Her laughter was soft, almost shy, as if it had been tucked away for a long time. She covered her mouth for a moment, shaking her head. "You're quite persistent for a stranger, you know that?"

I leaned back, letting the warmth of her laugh wash over me. "Persistence is just curiosity dressed up in nicer clothes," I said lightly. "And right now, I'm very curious about you."

She tilted her head, studying me as if trying to decide whether I was genuine or just another smooth talker. "Curiosity can be dangerous, you know," she said, her voice teasing but with a hint of caution underneath.

"True," I said, nodding. "But it can also lead to the most unexpected discoveries." I glanced at the notebook she had placed on the table beside her. "Like whatever it is you've been scribbling in there."

Her eyes darted to the notebook, and she instinctively placed her hand over it. "Just… thoughts," she said quickly. "Nothing worth sharing."

"Thoughts are always worth sharing," I said, leaning forward slightly. "Especially from someone who used to craft entire worlds with words."

Her smile faded a little, and her gaze dropped to the coffee cup in her hands. She ran her thumb along its rim, as if grounding herself in the moment. "Used to," she echoed softly. "That's the key phrase."

"Why not anymore?" I asked, my tone gentler now. "Why stop creating something that clearly meant so much to you?"

She hesitated, and for a moment, I thought she wouldn't answer. But then she sighed, her shoulders sagging slightly. "Sometimes the things we love most become the things that hurt us the deepest," she said. "And when that happens, walking away feels like the only way to survive."

Her words struck something deep within me. I wanted to tell her I understood, that her words had once been my lifeline, but I couldn't risk revealing myself yet. Instead, I said, "But does walking away really help? Or does it just leave you with an ache that never goes away?"

Her eyes met mine again, and for the first time, I saw a flicker of something raw and vulnerable. "Maybe," she said after a long pause. "But sometimes it's better to feel the ache than to keep bleeding."

I wanted to reach across the table, to tell her she didn't have to feel that way anymore, but I held back. This wasn't the time for confessions. Not yet.

"Fair enough," I said, leaning back and letting the silence settle between us. "But if it's worth anything, I think the world could use more of your words. Even if it's just one person's world."

Her lips parted slightly, as though she wanted to say something, but the barista's voice interrupted us. "Seraphine! Can you help me with the backroom inventory?"

She blinked, startled, and then stood up abruptly. "I—I have to go," she said, almost apologetically. "Thank you for the coffee."

Before I could say anything, she grabbed her notebook and hurried off toward the back of the café. I watched her go, my heart pounding in my chest.

She had said her name aloud. Seraphine.

It felt like hearing a symphony after years of silence.

I sat there for a long moment, staring at the empty chair across from me. I should have been content just seeing her, hearing her voice, but the ache in my chest told me I needed more.

I slipped my hand into my coat, pulling out the book she had written—the one that had brought me to this moment. My fingers brushed against its worn cover as I opened it to a page I knew by heart.

"If our words could find each other, maybe we can too."

And for the first time in a while, the words felt like they'd been brought back to life.

## 20
## Alasdair

When I got home, my legs felt like they were made of lead. My head was still spinning, replaying the evening over and over again. The sound of her voice, the way she talked—it was all too much and yet, not enough. I needed more, needed answers, but all I had was the lingering scent of coffee and the memory of her guarded smile.

Albert was sprawled out on the couch, flipping through channels with the kind of lazy precision that only he could manage. He glanced up as I walked in, his brows knitting together when he saw my face.

"You look like you've seen a ghost," he said, tossing the remote aside. "What happened?"

I dropped my coat on the nearest chair and ran a hand through my hair, pacing the length of the room like a caged animal. "It's her," I said finally, the words tumbling out of me. "Albert, I found her."

His expression shifted from confusion to surprise, and then to something bordering on concern. "What do you mean you 'found her'? Seraphine?"

"Yes," I said, turning to face him. "She was there. At the coffee shop. Sitting right in front of me, Albert. I talked to her."

"You talked to her?" His tone was disbelieving. "Like, actual words? Not just staring at her from a distance like some weirdo?"

"Yes, I talked to her," I snapped, though I knew I deserved the jab. "She was sitting there with that red notebook the librarian mentioned. I bought her coffee. But I couldn't tell her my name. And she works there, Albert. She's not just a customer—she works there."

Albert leaned forward, his elbows resting on his knees as he studied me. "Okay, hold on. Let me get this straight. You found Seraphine, the woman you've been obsessing over for years, and instead of telling her who you are, you... what? Bought her coffee and made small talk?"

"I didn't tell her," I admitted, sinking into the chair opposite him. "She didn't recognise me, and I didn't want to push it. I wanted to see if I could get her to open up first. To understand why she stopped writing, why she disappeared."

Albert groaned, dragging a hand down his face. "You're unbelievable, you know that? You've spent years chasing after this woman, and when you finally find her, you play it cool like you're in some kind of spy movie?"

"I couldn't just drop it on her!" I argued. "What was I supposed to say? 'Hi, I'm the guy who's been obsessing over your books and searching for you for years'? That would've gone over well."

"Well, what now?" he asked, crossing his arms. "Are you planning to stalk her until she magically figures it out?"

I glared at him, but his words hit too close to home. "I don't know," I admitted, slumping back in the chair. "I don't even know if she'd want to see me if she knew. But, Albert, she's not the person I imagined. She's... she's tired. Worn out. It's like there's this wall around her, and I don't know how to get past it."

Albert was silent for a moment, his expression softening. "Maybe she's tired because she's been through her own version of hell," he said. "You ever think about that? You're not the only one who's been carrying this weight, Alasdair. Maybe she's got her own scars."

His words hung in the air, heavy and undeniable. I had spent so long imagining her as this ethereal, untouchable figure that I hadn't considered the possibility that she might be just as broken as I was.

"So what do I do?" I asked. "How do I even begin to reach her?"

Albert leaned back, rubbing his chin thoughtfully. "You've got two options," he said. "You can keep playing the long game, slowly getting to know her as a stranger, or you can be honest. Tell her who you are, why you're here, and let her decide what happens next."

"Honesty," I muttered, the word feeling foreign and uncomfortable on my tongue. "That's easier said than done."

"Yeah, well, so is sitting here and moping about it," Albert said, standing up and stretching. "Look, you've already taken the hardest step—you found her. Now it's up to you to figure out how to keep her from slipping away again."

He clapped me on the shoulder as he walked past, leaving me alone with my thoughts.

The next day, I couldn't resist. I told myself I needed coffee, but we both knew it was more than that. The morning was cold, the kind that seeps into your bones, but my chest felt oddly warm, anticipation crackling like static in the air. I found myself at the café again, standing at the counter before I even realised I'd made the trip.

She was there, her copper-red hair pulled back into a loose bun, a few stray strands framing her face. Her apron was slightly crooked, and there was a smudge of flour on her forearm, as if she'd been baking something earlier. She looked... real. Not the ethereal, untouchable figure from my imagination, but someone grounded, someone trying to navigate her own chaos.

I leaned against the counter, my heart thumping in my chest. "Two cups of espresso, please."

She glanced up, her lips quirking into a polite smile. "I'm alright, sir. I'll just get you one."

I raised an eyebrow, feigning surprise. "Your customer asks for two, and you give them one? That's a risky move. Don't you think you might get fired for that?"

Her smile widened, a soft laugh escaping her lips as she sighed in mock defeat. "Alright, alright," she said, throwing her hands up in surrender. "Two espressos coming right up. But don't say I didn't warn you when you're too jittery to hold a conversation."

"Who says I'm drinking both?" I countered, leaning a little closer. "Maybe I'm just trying to keep the barista from collapsing mid-shift."

She shot me a look, half-amused and half-suspicious. "Oh, so now you're worried about my well-being? Very considerate, sir."

"It's not worry," I said with a smirk. "It's strategy. If you pass out, who's going to make my coffee?"

Her laugh was genuine this time, the kind that filled the small café like music. "You've got a point," she said, grabbing two cups and starting the espresso machine. "But don't think this means I'm making it a habit. Next time, you're sticking to one."

As she worked, I watched her, my nerves slowly giving way to something softer. There was a rhythm to her movements, grace that hinted at the person she used to be. But there was also a tension in her shoulders, a tiredness she couldn't hide.

When she placed the two steaming cups on the counter, she hesitated, her gaze flicking to me. "You always order coffee for two?" she asked lightly, though there was a hint of curiosity in her tone.

"Only when the company's worth it," I replied, sliding one cup toward her. "Care to join me? Or is that against company policy too?"

Her cheeks flushed slightly, and for a moment, I thought she might refuse. But then she glanced at the empty café, her lips curving into a soft smile. "I suppose I can take a break," she said, untying her apron and stepping out from behind the counter.

I carried the cups to a corner table, her footsteps soft behind me. As we sat down, the buzz of the espresso machine faded into the background, leaving just the two of us in the warm glow of the café. She wrapped her hands around the cup, her fingers tapping absently against the ceramic.

"So," she said, breaking the silence, "what brings you back here? Two days in a row seems a bit excessive for coffee, don't you think?"

I shrugged, meeting her gaze. "Maybe it's not about the coffee."

"Not about the coffee?" she repeated, her voice light, but I caught the edge of nervousness beneath it. She tilted her head slightly, studying me. "So what is it about then?"

I leaned back in my chair, feigning casualness, though my heart was racing. "Maybe I just enjoy the atmosphere. Or maybe," I added, lowering my voice a notch, "I wanted to see if the barista with the best espresso-making skills in town was real or just a rumour."

Her lips twitched, the corners pulling up into a reluctant smile. "Flattery doesn't work on me, you know."

"Not flattery. Truth." I sipped my coffee, letting the silence stretch for a beat. "But if I'm honest, you looked like you needed the company yesterday. I thought I'd check in."

She blinked, clearly caught off guard. "That's… kind of you," she said slowly, her voice softening. She took a sip of her own coffee, the cup hiding her expression for a moment. "Though most people don't make a habit of looking out for strangers."

"I'm not most people," I said, offering her a small smile. "And besides, sometimes strangers are easier to talk to than friends. No expectations, no judgments. Just a conversation over coffee."

Her fingers tightened around the cup, and I saw something flash in her eyes—recognition, maybe, or the memory of words she had written once upon a time. Words that had lived in my head for years.

"Maybe," she murmured, her gaze dropping to her cup. "But strangers also don't know when to stop asking questions."

I laughed softly. "Fair point. No hard questions today, I promise."

"Good." She smiled again, but it didn't reach her eyes. She took another sip of her coffee, her movements slower now, more thoughtful. "So, what do you do?"

"What I do depends on the day. Lately, it seems I've been wandering around, trying to make sense of things."

Her brow furrowed. "That's not much of an answer."

"Maybe not," I admitted. "But it's honest. What about you? What's a writer like you doing in a place like this?"

She stiffened slightly, her grip on the cup tightening again. "I told you yesterday—I'm not a writer anymore."

"Once a writer, always a writer," I countered, echoing my words from the day before. "You can't just stop being who you are."

Her gaze flickered to mine, sharp and unyielding. "Sometimes, you don't have a choice."

There it was again—the wall she kept so carefully built. I could see it in her posture, the way she leaned back slightly, as if to put more distance between us.

"What if you did? What if you could choose?"

She looked away, her fingers tracing the edge of the cup. "Life doesn't always work like that."

"Life rarely works the way we want it to," I said, leaning forward slightly, "but that doesn't mean we stop trying."

She let out a soft, humourless laugh, shaking her head. "You're awfully philosophical for someone who just came in for coffee."

"Maybe coffee brings out the philosopher in me," I said with a grin, trying to lighten the mood. "Or maybe I'm just curious about the person behind the notebook."

Her eyes snapped back to mine, and for a moment, I thought I'd gone too far. But instead of snapping at me or walking away, she surprised me.

"What is it you want to know?" she asked.

Everything, I thought. Every reason why you disappeared. Every piece of you I've only been able to guess at through your words. But instead, I smiled and said, "Why did you stop writing?"

She stilled, her expression unreadable. For a moment, I thought she wouldn't answer. But then she sighed, her shoulders slumping slightly.

"Because I thought," she said softly, "I found my poet."

## 21
## Alasdair

Her words floated in the air like the final note of a haunting melody, quiet yet deafening. My heart raced, my thoughts spiralling as I tried to grasp what she meant. She thought she found her poet? Who was she referring to? What had happened to make her stop believing?

Before I could respond, she shook her head and gave a dismissive laugh. "But that was a long time ago," she added quickly, waving her hand as if to push the memory away. "We all grow out of silly notions eventually."

"Silly?" I asked, tilting my head. "You don't strike me as someone who writes out of silly notions. Your words—" I stopped myself, catching the slip just in time. I couldn't let her know I'd read them. Not yet. "Writing like yours—well, I'd imagine it comes from something real."

Her eyes narrowed slightly. "You don't know anything about my writing," she said cautiously, her tone cool.

"You're right," I said quickly, backtracking. "I don't. I just meant... I don't think someone like you would pour themselves into something that didn't matter."

Her expression softened slightly, but the guarded look in her eyes remained. She leaned back in her chair, cradling her coffee cup like it was a shield. "Maybe it mattered too much," she said after a pause, her voice so low I almost missed it.

I studied her for a moment, weighing my next words carefully. "What happened?" I asked gently.

She gave me a long, measured look, as though deciding whether I was worth the effort of answering. Then she shrugged, her lips twisting into a bitter smile. "I made the mistake of believing in something. And when it all fell apart, so did I."

Her words hit me like a punch to the chest, but I kept my face neutral, letting her speak. This was her story, and I couldn't let my own emotions get in the way. Not yet.

"So, you stopped?" I asked softly. "Stopped writing, stopped believing?"

"That's not why I stopped writing. I thought I could finally be a poem. But the dream seems too out of reach now." she said, her voice sharp now, defensive.

"It sounds more like you gave up."

Her eyes snapped to mine, and for a moment, I saw a flicker of anger. Good. Anger meant passion. It meant she still cared, no matter how much she tried to convince herself otherwise.

"You don't know what you're talking about," she said flatly.

"Maybe I don't," I admitted. "But I know what it's like to lose something that matters. To feel like you're drowning and the only way to stay afloat is to let go of everything."

Her gaze wavered, the anger in her eyes fading into something softer, more vulnerable. She looked down, her lips pressing into a thin line.

"But you didn't drown," I added softly. "You're still here."

She let out a short, humourless laugh. "Barely."

"Barely is still enough," I said. "Enough to try again. Enough to write again."

Her head lifted, and for the first time, she looked at me like she was really seeing me—not just a stranger in a café, but someone who understood. Someone who cared.

"Why do you even care?" she asked. "You don't know me."

I held her gaze, choosing my words carefully. "Maybe I don't know you," I said slowly, "but I know what it feels like to need someone to remind you of who you are."

Her breath hitched, and for a moment, I thought she might cry. But then she blinked, the moment passing as quickly as it had come. She straightened in her chair, her guard snapping back into place.

"I appreciate the sentiment," she said, her tone cool again, "but it's not that simple."

"Nothing worth it ever is," I said, refusing to back down.

She stared at me for a long moment. Then she stood, her chair scraping softly against the floor.

"Thank you for the coffee," she said, her voice polite but distant. "But I should get back to work."

I didn't stop her this time. I simply watched as she walked back to the counter, her red hair catching the light like a flame. As she disappeared behind the counter, I leaned back in my chair and let out a long breath.

This wasn't over. Not by a long shot.

I sat there for a while, staring at the empty space where she had been sitting. The brief exchange had cracked something open—something I wasn't sure I was ready to face, but something that I couldn't ignore anymore.

I ran my fingers along the edge of the coffee cup, the warmth still lingering, a reminder of the connection that had sparked between us. For a moment, I considered leaving. Maybe I should just let it go, accept that some stories were never meant to be told, some people never meant to be understood.

But I couldn't.

I stood, paying for my coffee before I headed to the door, but as I stepped into the cool evening air, I hesitated.

I had to go back. Not because I was trying to fix anything, but because the silence between us wasn't enough. I needed more. I needed to understand her, to see her break past those walls she kept so carefully constructed.

I made my way back to the café the next day, my heart hammering in my chest. This time, I was determined to keep the conversation going. No more tiptoeing around. No more pretences. If she wouldn't talk about the past, then I would give her something to believe in now.

As I entered the familiar door, I saw her behind the counter, her back turned as she prepared a drink. I took a deep breath, trying to calm the nervous energy thrumming inside me, and walked over to the counter.

"Two cups of espresso, please," I said.

She looked up, the surprise flickering in her eyes before she quickly masked it with her usual professional smile. "Coming right up."

I leaned against the counter, glancing around the space. "I hope you're not getting tired of me."

She laughed softly, the sound light but slightly strained. "It's only been a couple of days."

"True," I said, watching her as she worked. "But that's enough time to form an opinion, don't you think?"

Her eyes met mine for a brief second, then she turned back to her task. She placed the cups in front of me with a practiced motion.

"I'll make sure I have an opinion by tomorrow," she said dryly, handing me the cups.

I took them, but instead of leaving, I placed them on the counter and slid onto one of the stools. "I'm not going anywhere this time."

She sighed, her fingers tapping lightly on the counter as she watched me. "You really don't give up, do you?"

"Nope," I replied, meeting her gaze with a determined smile. "Not when I think there's more to you than what meets the eye."

She shifted uncomfortably but didn't walk away. "And what exactly do you think is behind the eyes?" she asked, her tone more guarded now.

"Someone who's lost but still looking," I said, leaning in a little. "Someone who stopped writing because they didn't know how to keep going."

Her breath caught, and for a moment, I thought she might say something, but instead, she turned away, gathering a few napkins. The silence stretched between us, and I realised I'd pushed too far again. She wasn't ready to open up.

But I wouldn't give up. I couldn't.

"You're right," I said softly, breaking the silence. "I don't know you. But I'm willing to."

She looked back at me then, her eyes searching my face, perhaps wondering if I truly understood or if I was just another stranger trying to break through. I saw the hesitation in her eyes.

"I know you're not ready," I continued. "But when you are, I'll be here. To listen. No questions. No judgments."

She turned back to the counter, moving slowly.

"Maybe," she said under her breath. "Maybe."

I smiled, even though she couldn't see it. I didn't need her to say anything right now. But one day, I hoped she would.

I stayed at the counter for a while, watching her work, the rhythm of her movements deliberate yet distant, like someone trying to lose themselves in the mundane. She was avoiding me now, I could tell, but not in the way that pushed people away entirely. It was a careful sort of distance, as though she wasn't ready for anything but didn't want me to leave, either.

The café had a few scattered patrons, but none paid her much attention. I noticed the way she kept her eyes on her work, how her hands moved with precision even when her mind seemed elsewhere. The red notebook wasn't visible today, and I wondered if she had hidden it after yesterday's interaction.

I wasn't sure why I didn't leave. Maybe it was the hopeless hope that she'd come back, that the silence between us might break just a little more.

Eventually, the café began to empty. A couple in the corner finished their drinks and left, the man with the laptop packed up his things, and soon it was just the two of us. She finished wiping the counters, her back to me, and I finally stood to leave.

"Thanks for the coffee," I said, pushing the empty cup toward her.

She turned slightly, her eyes meeting mine for a second before she nodded. "Anytime."

I lingered, wanting to say something more but knowing it wouldn't help. Instead, I gave her a small smile and walked out into the evening air.

The next day, I returned again.

This time, I didn't even pretend to order. I sat at the same table as before, near the window, and waited. She spotted me almost immediately but didn't come over. Instead, she continued working, her movements a little stiffer than usual, like she was hyper-aware of my presence.

Minutes passed, and when the café quieted again, she finally approached, a cup of coffee in her hand.

"You know, most people at least pretend to look at the menu," she said, setting the cup down in front of me. Her tone was light, but her eyes held a guarded curiosity.

"Most people aren't here for the coffee," I replied, leaning back and crossing my legs.

She raised an eyebrow, crossing her arms. "Still not about the coffee?"

"Still not," I said, smiling. "But I promise I'm not here to bother you."

"You're not doing a great job of that," she muttered, though her lips twitched like she was trying not to smile.

I tapped the edge of the cup. "Maybe I just wanted to return the favour. Yesterday, you listened. Today, I'm here to do the same."

She blinked, clearly caught off guard. "What makes you think I need someone to listen?"

"Because everyone does," I said simply.

Her arms tightened around herself, and I thought she might walk away. But then she pulled out the chair across from me and sat down, her posture cautious but not entirely closed off.

"You're persistent," she said, her tone more curious than annoyed now.

"It's one of my better qualities," I replied, smiling.

She sighed, shaking her head slightly, but she didn't leave. Instead, she looked at me, her gaze sharp and assessing.

"So, what's your story then?" she asked. "You keep coming here, asking questions, acting like you've got me all figured out. But what about you? What's the big mystery?"

I hesitated. For all my planning, I hadn't expected the conversation to turn on me so quickly.

"I'm just someone looking for answers," I said finally. "And maybe a little closure."

Her eyes narrowed slightly, and I could see the gears turning in her mind. "Closure? Sounds heavy."

"It is," I admitted. "But sometimes you have to go through the heavy stuff to find what you're looking for."

She looked away, her fingers drumming lightly on the table. "And have you found it yet?"

"Not yet," I said softly, my gaze steady on her. "But I think I'm getting closer."

For a moment, she didn't respond. Then, with a small shake of her head, she stood.

"Well," she said in a brisk tone, "I hope you find what you're looking for."

Before I could reply, she turned and walked back to the counter, leaving me sitting there with more questions than answers.

But this time, I didn't feel discouraged. Because as guarded as she was, as much as she tried to keep me at arm's length, I could see it—the crack in her defences, the part of her that wanted to let someone in.

And I wasn't going to stop trying.

## 22
## Alasdair

The next evening, I found myself leaning against the streetlamp outside the café, the soft glow illuminating the cobblestone path. The air was carrying the faint scent of roasted coffee beans from the café's vents. I checked my watch—it was almost closing time.

I hadn't planned on waiting for her, not consciously at least. But something about yesterday's conversation stayed, an unfinished thread I couldn't ignore.

The lights inside the café dimmed slightly, signalling the end of her shift. Moments later, the door opened, and she stepped out, tying her scarf around her neck.

She didn't notice me at first. Her head was down, her hair glowing faintly under the lamplight, and she looked as though she were lost in thought.

"Long day?" I asked, breaking the silence.

She was startled, her hand instinctively tightening around her bag as she looked up. Her eyes softened when she saw it was me, though her expression quickly turned wary.

"You again?" she said, her tone a mix of curiosity and exasperation.

"Me again," I said with a small smile. "I figured I'd walk you home."

She raised an eyebrow. "Do you always wait outside cafés for people to finish their shifts?"

"Only when they're as interesting as you," I teased lightly. "But no, not usually."

She sighed, shaking her head. "You're persistent, I'll give you that."

"It's a good quality, remember?" I said, echoing my words from the day before.

She chuckled softly, her breath visible in the cold air. "Alright, mystery man. Let's walk. But just so you know, I don't live far."

"I'm not walking you home," I said, stepping beside her as we began down the street.

She glanced at me, confused. "Then where are we going?"

"You'll see."

She hesitated, her pace slowing. "I'm not a fan of surprises."

"It's not a surprise," I reassured her. "Just a place I think you might like."

She studied me for a moment before nodding reluctantly. "Alright. Lead the way."

The library stood quiet and grand at the end of the street, its imposing doors framed by ivy creeping along the stone walls. The warm glow of light spilled through the tall windows, making it look inviting despite the late hour.

She stopped in her tracks as soon as it came into view.

"The library?" she asked, her tone soft but tinged with disbelief.

"I thought it might feel familiar," I said, gesturing toward the entrance.

Her lips parted as if to say something, but she closed them again with an unreadable expression. After a long moment, she took a tentative step forward.

Inside, the library was nearly empty, save for a few lingering readers and a librarian shelving books. The hum of whispered voices created a cocoon of peace.

I watched as she walked ahead, her eyes scanning the towering bookshelves. Her hand brushed the spines of the books as though she were greeting old friends.

"Why here?" she finally asked, turning back to me.

"Because it's where stories live," I said. "And I think stories are where you belong."

She didn't respond right away, her gaze lingering on mine before drifting back to the shelves.

"It's been a long time since I've been in a library," she admitted.

"Too long," I said, stepping closer. "I can tell."

She gave me a look—half-annoyed, half-amused. "You're too good at that."

"At what?"

"Reading people," she said, a faint smile tugging at her lips.

"It's a skill," I replied, shrugging. "But you're not exactly hard to read."

She tilted her head, her expression shifting to something more serious. "You think you know me?"

"I think I want to," I said honestly.

Her gaze held mine for a long moment, and for the first time, I saw the hint of something breaking through her guarded exterior. Not trust, not yet—but maybe the possibility of it.

She turned away, her fingers lingering on a book's spine. "So," she said, her voice lighter, "are you going to pick a book, or am I the only one browsing?"

I smiled, sensing the change in her mood. "Let's pick one together," I suggested.

She looked at me over her shoulder, a flicker of curiosity in her eyes. "Together?"

"Why not?" I said, stepping beside her. "We'll find something worth reading. Maybe even something worth remembering."

"Alright, mystery man," she said, reaching for a book. "Let's see what we find."

And just like that, the walls she had built so carefully seemed a little less impenetrable.

We spent the next hour wandering the aisles of the library, our conversation ebbing and flowing as naturally as the rustle of pages around us. She moved with reverence, her fingers brushing along the spines of books.

Occasionally, she'd pull one out, flip through the pages, and then set it back with a soft smile or a sigh. I watched her carefully, noticing the way her eyes softened when she found something familiar or the way her lips twitched at an amusing title.

"So," I said, breaking the comfortable silence, "what's the verdict? Found anything worth remembering yet?"

She turned to me, holding up a book with a faded red cover. "This one," she said with excitement.

I leaned closer, reading the title aloud. "The Collected Poems of Rainer Maria Rilke."

She nodded, her expression thoughtful. "Rilke has always been special to me. His words feel like they're written in the margins of your own soul."

"Sounds like he's in good company, then," I said with a smile, earning a blush from her.

"What about you?" she asked, shifting the attention back to me. "What's your choice?"

I shrugged, scanning the shelves. "I'm still looking. But I think I'll know it when I see it."

She arched an eyebrow. "You're either incredibly intuitive or just stalling."

"Maybe both," I admitted, grinning.

Eventually, my eyes landed on a slim, unassuming volume tucked between two larger tomes. The title was embossed in gold: The Art of Waiting.

"This one," I said, pulling it out and showing her.

Her expression softened as she read the title. "That's a little poetic, don't you think?"

"Maybe," I said, running my fingers over the cover. "But I think some things are worth waiting for."

We found a quiet corner of the library, an alcove with two worn armchairs and a small table. She settled into one of the chairs, tucking her legs beneath her and opening the Rilke book. I took the other, flipping through 'The Art of Waiting' but only half-reading the words.

The silence between us was comfortable, broken only by the occasional turn of a page or the soft hum of the library's heating system.

"Why did you really bring me here?"

I looked up, meeting her gaze. "Because I thought it might remind you of something important."

She frowned slightly, her fingers toying with the corner of a page. "And what's that?"

"That words don't just belong to the person who writes them," I said. "They belong to the people who carry them. And I think you've been carrying words for a long time without letting them go."

Her breath hitched, and she quickly looked down, pretending to focus on the book in her lap.

"You don't know me," she said softly.

"Maybe not," I agreed. "But I've read enough to recognise when someone is trying to disappear between the lines."

She didn't respond, her grip on the book tightening. I wanted to say more, to press her, but I knew better than to push too hard.

Instead, I leaned back in my chair, giving her the space to process.

We stayed there until the library's closing announcement crackled over the speakers. As we walked back to the entrance, she clutched the Rilke book tightly, her fingers curling around its edges like a lifeline.

"Thank you," she said as we stepped out into the cool night air.

"For what?" I asked, falling into step beside her.

"For not asking too many questions," she said. "And for letting me just... be."

I smiled back, tucking my hands into my coat pockets. "Anytime."

We walked in silence for a while, the city quiet around us. When we reached the street corner where we'd part ways, she paused, looking up at me.

"I don't usually do this," she said, her voice tinged with uncertainty. "But... do you want to come back tomorrow? For another coffee?"

It was such a simple question, yet it carried so much with it.

"I'd like that," I said, trying to keep my tone light even as my chest swelled with hope.

She nodded. "Okay. See you tomorrow, then."

And with that, she turned and walked away, her red hair under the streetlights looked like a fading ember. I stood there for a moment, watching her disappear into the night, my heart pounding with the realisation that, for the first time in years, she was starting to let me in.

## 23
## Alasdair

The next day, I arrived at the café a little earlier than usual. The morning air carried a crisp bite, and the streets were still waking up, scattered with a few early risers and the sound of distant traffic. I stood outside, watching through the window as Seraphine moved about behind the counter, her motions fluid and practiced.

She hadn't noticed me yet, which gave me a moment to take her in. There was something calming about seeing her in her element, the way she interacted with the occasional customer or adjusted her apron absentmindedly.

When the morning rush subsided, I pushed open the door, the bell overhead jingling softly. She glanced up, and for a brief moment, her expression flickered with something I couldn't quite place—surprise? Relief?

"Two cups of coffee?" she asked, a small smile tugging at her lips as I approached the counter.

"Only one today," I said, leaning casually against the counter. "I wouldn't want to overwork you."

She chuckled softly. "I'll manage."

While she prepared my coffee, I noticed the faint shadows under her eyes. She was smiling, but there was a weight behind it, as though she were carrying something unseen.

"Late night with Rilke?" I asked as she handed me the cup.

Her smile faltered for a split second before she nodded. "Something like that."

"Good read?"

"Always," she said, her tone lighter now. "He has a way of making you feel like he understands everything you're afraid to say out loud."

I raised my cup in mock toast. "Here's to Rilke, then."

She laughed, shaking her head. "You're insufferable, you know that?"

"Yet, here I am, being invited back for coffee," I teased.

Her cheeks flushed, but she didn't respond. Instead, she reached for a nearby rag, wiping the counter in small, deliberate circles.

"Actually," I said, setting my coffee down, "I was thinking we could do something different today."

She raised an eyebrow, curious. "Different how?"

"You've been serving coffee all week," I said. "How about I take you somewhere for a change?"

She hesitated, her fingers tightening around the rag. "I don't know... I have my shift—"

"After your shift," I interrupted gently. "No pressure. Just think about it."

I stayed quiet, letting her make the decision.

Finally, she sighed, a reluctant smile forming. "Fine. But if this is another trip to the library, you're going to have to get more creative."

I grinned. "Noted."

When her shift ended, we met outside the café. She had traded her apron for a simple cardigan, her hair falling loosely over her shoulders.

"So," she said, crossing her arms and giving me a mock-serious look. "Where are we going?"

"You'll see," I said, starting down the street.

We walked in comfortable silence, the city around us slowly transitioning into the golden hues of late afternoon. I led her to a small, tucked-away bookshop that specialised in rare and used books.

Her eyes widened when we stepped inside, the scent of aged paper and ink wrapping around us like a warm embrace. Shelves stretched to the ceiling, crammed with titles in every imaginable genre.

"This," I said, gesturing to the space, "is where I come when I need to get lost."

She turned to me. "You brought me here to get lost?"

"Not just lost," I said, smiling. "To find something worth holding onto."

She wandered through the aisles, her fingers trailing over the spines. Occasionally, she'd pull out a book, examine it, and then place it back with a thoughtful hum. I followed a few steps behind, giving her space to explore.

Eventually, she stopped at a shelf labelled 'Poetry and Prose'. Her eyes lit up as she pulled out a small, leather-bound book.

"What did you find?" I asked, stepping closer.

She held it up, her smile tentative but genuine. "It's a collection of unpublished letters by Sylvia Plath."

"Impressive find," I said, leaning in to read the cover. "Are you going to get it?"

She hesitated, her fingers brushing over the cover. "Maybe."

"Maybe?"

She laughed softly. "I don't know. I feel like I've been avoiding books for so long, like they might remember all the things I've tried to forget."

"Books don't hold grudges," I said. "If anything, they're probably happy to have you back."

Her smile turned wistful, and for a moment, she looked almost at peace.

"Maybe," she said again, but this time, there was less doubt in her voice.

The walk back from the bookshop was mute but not uncomfortable. Seraphine clutched the leather-bound book close to her chest, her fingers absentmindedly tracing its edges. The golden light of the setting sun painted the street in soft hues, casting long shadows of trees swaying gently in the breeze.

"You're quiet," I said, breaking the silence as we passed a small park.

She glanced at me, her lips curving into a faint smile. "I'm thinking."

"About?"

"About how long it's been since I felt... normal," she admitted. "It's strange, isn't it? How something as simple as walking out of a bookshop can feel like a big step forward."

I matched her pace, shoving my hands into my coat pockets. "Maybe it's not about the bookshop. Maybe it's about letting yourself take that step."

She didn't respond immediately. Instead, her gaze drifted toward a group of children chasing each other in the park, their laughter carrying over to us.

"You make it sound easy," she said softly.

"It's not," I said. "But you're doing it anyway. That's what matters."

We stopped at the edge of the park, where a wrought iron bench sat under a sprawling oak tree. Seraphine hesitated before sitting down, the book resting on her lap.

I took the spot beside her, letting the sounds of the city fade into the background. She stared at the book in her hands.

"I used to think books had all the answers," she said. "When I was younger, I believed every problem could be solved if I just found the right words."

"And now?"

"Now," she said with a bitter laugh, "I'm not so sure. Words feel heavy. Like they've betrayed me somehow."

"Words don't betray," I said gently. "But they can feel like strangers when you've been away from them for too long."

Her eyes flicked to mine, searching for something in my expression. "Do you always talk like this? Like you're trying to pull the answers out of people?"

I chuckled. "Only when I'm with someone worth figuring out."

She rolled her eyes, but the faintest blush crept into her cheeks. "You're relentless, you know that?"

"It's been said." I leaned back against the bench, tilting my head toward the sky. "But seriously, you don't have to carry all of it alone. Sometimes, sharing the weight makes it easier to move forward."

She was quiet for a long moment, her gaze fixed on the book in her lap. Then, almost imperceptibly, she nodded.

"Maybe," she murmured. "But I wouldn't even know where to start."

"How about here?" I suggested. "With me. No expectations, no judgments. Just... whatever you want to share."

She looked at me again, her eyes softer now, less guarded. "You're really not going to give up, are you?"

I smiled. "Not a chance."

"Alright," she said, leaning back against the bench. "But don't say I didn't warn you. My story's not exactly a happy one."

"I didn't come here for happy," I said simply. "I came here for the truth."

And with that, she began to speak.

## 24
## Alasdair

"I'm in love with someone," she said softly.

"And?" I prompted, leaning in slightly.

"And…" She hesitated, her gaze dropping to her hands clasped tightly in her lap. "He might not be real."

I blinked, caught off guard. "What do you mean?"

She let out a nervous laugh, shaking her head as if to dismiss the absurdity of her own words. "I mean… he doesn't exist. Not in the way people are supposed to. Not in the flesh-and-blood, walk-around-on-this-earth kind of way."

I tilted my head, trying to understand. "So, who is he then? A dream? A memory?"

She smiled faintly, a touch of sadness in her expression. "No. He's... someone I never met. And yet, he feels more real to me than anyone I've ever met."

"Through books?" I asked cautiously.

Her eyes widened, the colour draining slightly from her face. "How do you know that?"

I hesitated for a moment, trying to keep my tone light. "I mean... you're an author," I said with a small shrug. "It's not that much of a stretch to think you'd create someone so vivid, someone who feels real enough to love."

She studied me carefully, her fingers toying with the edge of her sleeve. "That's... an oddly specific guess."

"Not really," I said. "Writers pour themselves into their characters. Sometimes, the lines blur."

She let out a soft laugh, though it was tinged with something vulnerable. "You make it sound so normal. Like it's not completely insane to fall in love with someone you made up."

"Not insane," I said, meeting her gaze. "Just human."

"Maybe," she murmured. "But it doesn't feel human. It feels... impossible. Like trying to hold onto a dream when you're already awake."

"But dreams have a way of staying with us, don't they? Even when we wake up, parts of them linger. Maybe the person you love isn't just in your head."

Her gaze snapped to mine, a flicker of something—hope, maybe—crossing her face. "What do you mean?"

"I mean, sometimes the people we write about aren't entirely made up. Maybe he's someone you've already met, someone you saw once, or even someone you wished existed so much that he found a way to feel real."

"I feel like I've created a version of him in my mind, one that doesn't really exist."

"Why do you feel that way?"

"I've been searching for him, hoping to find even a trace of the person I remember. But I keep coming up empty. And the more I search, the more I realise… maybe it was all just a dream. But there's still this flicker of hope that refuses to fade. It's like I'm trying to convince myself that it's over, but part of me still believes I can find him again."

"Maybe you already found him."

"I don't know," she muttered. "It's like I built him up to be something he never was, and now I'm stuck trying to find that illusion in the real world."

"May I know who he is?"

"He's a writer. We met between the lines, in the words we shared that never needed to be spoken." She said, smiling. I didn't utter a word. I knew what she meant.

"It's like… we understood each other in a way that went beyond the surface. His words felt like mine, as if we were both searching for something we couldn't find in the real world, but there, in what we wrote, we found each other."

"So what made you stop?"

"I was fed up with the distance. I couldn't bear just existing in those words anymore. I needed to meet him in real life, to see if he was as real as I felt he was. So I broke off my engagement with my fiancé—the one who never really loved me, the one who was more like a placeholder than a partner. I fought with my family, who didn't understand, and I ran away from home. I ended up here, in this city, on a wild search to find him." I was shocked. For a moment, it felt like the world had paused.

"It can't be. It couldn't be me." I thought. But the more I listened, the more the pieces began to fall into place.

She did all that for me?

I couldn't believe it. I had never imagined—never even dared to hope—that someone would go to such lengths for me. To break off an engagement, to fight with her family, to abandon everything and chase a name, a dream, a me that she had built from words on a page.

I wanted to say something, but the words felt stuck, tangled in the weight of the revelation. My heart raced, and my mind struggled to make sense of it all.

She noticed my silence and hesitated. "I... I know it sounds crazy. Maybe it is. But I couldn't just sit back anymore. I had to know. Had to find out if what we had between those words could be real in the world outside of them."

I swallowed hard, finally managing to speak. "You really came all this way for someone you met through books? And you thought a city was all you needed?"

"I had a name, a city, a tiny thread to follow. It was all I had to go on, and I couldn't ignore it. I searched online, found the name of the city, and that was the only clue that felt real enough to hold onto.

So without thinking much about it, I packed my bags and flew here, to this unknown place. No plan, no real backup, just the hope that something, anything, would bring me closer to him."

I stared at her, trying to process everything she had just said. It felt like I was hearing a story from someone else, a surreal narrative that didn't fit with the life I knew. She had come all this way, on nothing but a name and a city, just to find me. The depth of her belief in something she couldn't even explain hung between us like an unspoken question.

"Isn't that... dangerous? I mean, you're just hoping to find someone in a city you barely know, based on nothing but a guess?"

She nodded. "Maybe it's reckless. Maybe it's foolish. But sometimes, you have to take those risks, don't you? Sometimes, you have to leap without knowing if the ground is going to catch you. Otherwise, you just stay stuck in the same place, wondering what could have been."

Her words hit me harder than I expected. They were filled with a kind of bravery that I wasn't sure I had. It was hard for me to imagine putting everything on the line for something so intangible. For someone like me, a person whose reality often felt more like a jumble of questions than answers, her certainty was almost foreign.

"I never thought I'd do something like this," she continued, her voice soft but steady. "But I couldn't keep pretending like the words we shared were just... nothing. Like they didn't mean anything. If I didn't follow that thread, I'd always wonder what might have been. And I wasn't willing to live with that."

"How long have you been here?" I asked.

"Two years."

"And how long do you plan to stay?"

"I don't know. Maybe… forever?" She looked up at me with teary eyes. Eyes that held hope and yet, they looked hopeless.

I couldn't form words. Noticing my actions, she continued speaking.

"You know what he said to me?" She smiled faintly through her cries. I just stared at her face, waiting for her to continue.

"Maybe I never met you," she proceeded. "but between the lines, where stories live and souls meet…"

I cut her off by continuing the line.

"I found you."

## 25
## Alasdair

She shot her head up, her eyes wide with disbelief.

"What did you just say?" she gasped, her breath coming in quick, shallow bursts.

"Between the lines, where stories live and souls meet, I found you." I repeated.

"How do you know that line?" she asked. I shrugged my shoulders.

She stared at me, her expression intense. "Tell me. Where did you hear that?" she asked again.

"I read it in a book," I said, meeting her gaze.

"Really?" She raised an eyebrow, skeptical. "It's from a very obscure book, though."

"Maybe. But you should continue what you were saying," I urged.

She stared at me for a moment, then began again. "There's more he said to me…"

I leaned in, captivated by the tension in her words. "What did he say?"

She looked down, as if finding the right words took effort, then lifted her gaze back to mine. "Maybe… you are my poem."

Her eyes locked onto mine as she recited the words.

"Unwritten, yet complete," she continued.

"A rhythm I've always felt but never heard,

A truth I was too afraid to claim." We recited the words together.


She gasped. Louder.

Covering her mouth with her palms, she widened her eyes again. "Have we met before?" She asked.

"Maybe we've met a thousand times before—in sentences, in stories, in lives that never made it to the page."

"Who… who are you exactly?" her eyes stared deep into my soul, her pupils flickering.

"Someone who you think is not real."

"What do you mean?"

"Oh! Look how stupid I am. We've been talking for days but I absolutely forgot to introduce myself. I'm Alasdair Davies. I was born and raised in this city."

She looked at me with her lips slightly parted. I noticed her lips to be trembling, which soon passed on to her hands. Something glistened in her eyes. In no time, a teardrop fell.

"Hey... are you okay?" I was dumbfounded, I didn't know what to do.

"Why didn't you tell me all this time?" She said in a broken voice.

"I wanted to make sure that it's me that you're searching for. I didn't want to pour my assumptions on you and make you stressed. I wanted to be sure first."

She wiped her tears quickly, as if embarrassed by her emotions, but they kept falling despite her efforts. "I can't believe this," she murmured, her voice quivering. "I came here with nothing but a name and a city. I searched and searched. I almost started to lose hope, and now, you're right in front of me."

I felt my chest tighten. "I didn't know how to tell you," I said softly. "When I realised it was me you were looking for, I... I needed to understand why. I needed to know if the connection you felt was real."

Her hands trembled as she lowered them from her face. "It was real," she said firmly. "It is real. I've lived with your words for years, Alasdair. They were my escape, my comfort, my everything. They were more than just stories—they were pieces of you, pieces I fell in love with."

Hearing her say that hit me harder than I expected. My own words, written long ago, had brought her here. And now, she was there in front of me, offering me her truth.

"I don't even know what to say. You left your entire life behind to find me. That's... more than I ever could've imagined."

She shifted closer, her voice trembling with a mix of hope and fear. "Tell me it wasn't all in my head. Tell me you felt it too. That you wrote those words because you were reaching for something—someone."

"I did write those words for someone," I said slowly. "I didn't know if it was me who she was writing for. But I hoped she did. And now… here you are."

Her breath hitched, and before I could say another word, she closed the gap between us, throwing her arms around me. The force of her embrace was both overwhelming and grounding, as if the universe had finally answered a question neither of us had dared to ask aloud.

For a moment, we stayed there, holding on to each other as though the world outside didn't exist. It felt surreal, but it also felt right—like two halves of a story finally coming together.

"I found you," she whispered against my shoulder, her voice thick with emotion. "After all this time, I found you."

"And I found you," I replied. "Between the lines, where stories live and souls meet, I found you too."

## 26

# Alasdair

"You don't know how much I love you, how much I've looked for you," she cried, her voice breaking as tears streaked down her cheeks. Her grip on my hands tightened, as if holding me physically would keep me from ever slipping away again.

I cupped her face gently, brushing away a tear with my thumb. "Me too," I whispered. "I've spent years trying to make sense of why you disappeared, why everything fell apart. And all I ever wanted to know was if you were okay."

Her gaze locked onto mine, unflinching and full of love. "And now we've found each other. After all these years, Alasdair, we're here. Together. What are we waiting for?"

"What do you mean?" I asked, though a part of me already knew where this was headed.

She took a shaky breath, determination flickering through her tears. "I can't wait any longer," she said firmly. "It's been eight years,

Alasdair. Eight years of being apart, of searching, of trying to find my way to you. Let's stop wasting time. Let's get married."

"Married?" The word tumbled out of my mouth, unsteady and hesitant, like a stone skipping across a still lake.

"Yes. It's time. We've waited long enough."

I stared at her, my heart racing in my chest. Part of me wanted to say yes immediately, to leap into a future where we didn't have to second-guess or hesitate. But another part held me back.

"No," I said, shaking my head slowly.

Her face fell, confusion and hurt crossing her features. "No?"

"It's not that I don't want to," I rushed to explain, my hands moving to hers again, desperate to hold onto her. "It's just… that's not possible."

I said, before gently shrugging her hand off mine. The warmth of her touch lingered for a moment, but I couldn't bring myself to meet her eyes again. Without another word, I stood up and walked away, each step feeling heavier than the last.

The sound of her sharp, uneven breaths followed me, a quiet plea that I tried to shut out but couldn't. My heart ached with every step, a silent war raging inside me between the love I couldn't deny and the fear I couldn't overcome.

When I reached my door, I paused, my hand hovering over the handle. For a split second, I thought about turning back. But I didn't. I opened the door, stepped in, and let it close behind me, leaving her alone in the dark.

The click of the door was deafening, cutting through the space like a final word neither of us wanted to say.

"Why is your face so pale?" Albert asked, his brow furrowed with concern.

"She asked me to marry her," I said between harsh breaths.

Albert's eyes widened. "Oh my God. Really?"

I nodded, my hands shoved deep into my pockets. "Yes."

"Then why do you look like someone just punched you in the gut?"

"I said no."

His jaw dropped. "What the hell? You what? Why would you do that?"

"Did you forget what the doctor said? It's serious, Albert. I can't drag her into this. I can't ruin her life like that."

Albert stared at me, disbelief etched into his face. "Ruin her life? Are you serious right now? She's not asking for a guarantee of forever—she's asking for you. You're the one she wants, not some perfect version of a future. Do you even realise what you've just done?"

"I know what I've done, Albert. And I hate myself for it. But this… this is the only way to protect her."

Albert shook his head, running a hand through his hair in frustration. "Protect her? That's the excuse you're going with? You're not protecting her, you're pushing her away. Do you really think that's what she wants?"

I clenched my fists, his words hitting me like a punch to the chest. "What else am I supposed to do?" I snapped. "Pretend like everything's fine? Pretend like I'm not a ticking time bomb? She deserves more than that—more than me."

Albert took a step closer, his voice softer now but no less firm. "What she deserves is the truth. Not you deciding for her what's best. You think you're being noble, but all you're doing is robbing her of the choice. Do you think she doesn't know what she's getting into? Do you think she doesn't want to fight this with you?"

I turned away, my shoulders sagging under the weight of it all. "You don't understand," I muttered.

"Don't I?" Albert's voice sharpened, cutting through my defences. "I get that you're scared. I get that this feels impossible. But running away isn't the answer. You've found someone who loves you, who's willing to stand by you no matter what—and you're throwing that away because of your pride."

"It's not pride," I said through gritted teeth, turning back to face him. "It's reality. The doctor was clear—there's no guarantee. How am I supposed to promise her a future when I don't even know if I have one?"

"No one gets guarantees, Alasdair. Not you, not her, not anyone. Life isn't about knowing how it ends—it's about what you do with the time you have. She's chosen you, despite everything. Don't you think she deserves the chance to decide how she spends her time, too?"

I looked down at the floor, the fight draining out of me as his words sank in. Deep down, I knew he was right. But the fear—the suffocating, paralysing fear—still loomed large.

"What if I hurt her, Albert?" I whispered.

Albert stepped closer, placing a hand on my shoulder. "You will. That's what love does sometimes. But you'll also make her happier than anyone else ever could. Isn't that worth the risk?"

I closed my eyes, the image of her face flashing in my mind—her smile, her tears, the way she'd looked at me when she asked the question I'd been too scared to answer.

"Do you think she'll forgive me?" My voice trembled.

Albert smiled faintly, giving my shoulder a reassuring squeeze. "She loves you, doesn't she? Go to her, Alasdair. Tell her the truth. And this time, don't run."

Without another word, I grabbed my coat and headed for the door, my heart pounding as I stepped into the night. It was time to fix what I'd broken. Time to face her. And this time, I wouldn't let fear win.

I rushed back to the park, my chest tightening with every step. The stillness of the night was amplifying the sound of my frantic breaths.

When I reached the spot where I had left her, my heart sank. The bench was empty, the space where she had sat now cold and desolate. I turned in a slow circle, scanning the area for any sign of her.

"Seraphine?" I called out, my voice echoing into the quiet. There was no answer, only the faint rustling of leaves in the wind.

I stood there for a moment, frozen by the crushing weight of regret. She had waited for me—of course, she had waited. And I hadn't been there.

I ran a hand through my hair, frustration and guilt tangling together in my chest. Why had I walked away in the first place? Why had I let my fear dictate everything?

Just as I was about to turn and leave, I spotted something on the ground near the bench. A scarf—hers. I picked it up, the fabric still warm from where it had rested on her shoulders.

Clutching it tightly, I looked around one last time, hoping against hope that she might still be nearby. But the park remained empty.

I pressed the scarf to my chest, a silent vow forming in my mind. Wherever she had gone, I would find her. And when I did, I would tell her everything—the truth, my fears, my love. This time, I wouldn't let her down.

With one last glance at the empty bench, I turned and walked into the night, the scarf clutched in my hand like a lifeline.

## 27
## Alasdair

The next day, I went to the café where she worked. I pushed through the door, the familiar jingle of the bell above signalling my arrival. My eyes immediately darted toward the counter, searching for her.

But she wasn't there.

I told myself she must be running late, that any moment she'd walk through the door, her hair slightly disheveled from the wind, that warm, soft smile on her lips. So I ordered a coffee and took a seat by the window, my gaze fixed on the entrance.

The hours stretched on, and the coffee grew cold in front of me. Still, she didn't come.

I convinced myself it was just a one-off, that something unexpected had come up. But when the next day came and she still wasn't there, a feeling of uneasiness started to form in my chest.

For the next two weeks, I went back every day, always at the same time, always hoping to see her. Each morning, I walked into the café with hope that would inevitably dim as the hours passed. I sat at the same table, ordered the same coffee, and waited.

The baristas started to notice, their curious glances lingering on me longer each day. One of them even approached me after a week. "Excuse me," she said hesitantly, her hands wiping a tray. "You've been coming here a lot. Are you waiting for someone?"

I hesitated, unsure how much to say. "Yeah," I admitted. "She used to work here. Red hair, quiet, always smiling… You know who I mean?"

The barista nodded, recognition flashing in her eyes. "Seraphine? She hasn't been in for a while now."

"Do you know why?" I asked.

She shook her head. "No, sorry. She didn't say much when she left."

"When she left?" The words hit me like a punch.

"Yeah," the barista said, her tone apologetic. "She didn't give notice or anything. Just stopped coming in. We thought maybe she moved or… I don't know."

I nodded, trying to hide the growing ache in my chest. "Thanks," I muttered, though the answer gave me none of the solace I had hoped for.

Every day after that, I came back, hoping that she'd show up, that I'd catch even a glimpse of her. But the weeks stretched on, and with each passing day, the hope I clung to began to feel more and more like a thread about to snap.

The café became a hollow space—a place filled with memories of her that I couldn't escape. Her laughter echoed in my mind, the way her hands moved when she poured coffee, the small, shy smiles she reserved just for me.

By the end of the second week, I sat at the table longer than usual, staring out the window. She was gone. Not just from the café, but from my life. And I had no idea where to find her.

Yet, even as I left that day, the ache in my chest didn't fade. Because no matter how hopeless it seemed, I knew I wasn't ready to stop looking.

The following morning, I woke up with a heaviness that felt like it was pressing me into the mattress. Two weeks. Two weeks of waiting, searching, and coming up empty. I stared at the ceiling, the faint light of dawn creeping in through the blinds, and wondered if I was fooling myself.

Maybe she didn't want to be found.

But the thought of giving up felt like admitting defeat—not just to myself, but to her. She had waited for me once, had fought for us, and I had let her down. The least I could do was keep trying.

So, I pulled myself out of bed and headed back to the café. This time, though, I wasn't going to sit and wait. I approached the counter, steeling myself as I addressed the barista who had spoken to me before.

"Excuse me," I said, trying to keep the desperation out of my voice. "Is there anyone here who might know where Seraphine went? A manager or someone?"

The barista frowned thoughtfully. "I don't think so. Like I said, she didn't really tell anyone much. But…" She hesitated.

"But what?" I pressed, leaning forward.

"She was close with Mrs. Ellis—the older woman who comes in every Thursday morning. They used to talk a lot. Maybe she knows something?"

My heart skipped a beat. It wasn't much, but it was something. "Thank you," I said, my voice firmer now.

The hours crawled by as I waited for Thursday to arrive. When the morning finally came, I was at the café before it even opened, pacing the sidewalk like a man possessed.

At exactly 9:00 AM, Mrs. Ellis arrived, her small frame wrapped in a wool coat. She carried a book under one arm and walked with a slow but deliberate pace.

I approached her cautiously, not wanting to startle her. "Mrs. Ellis?" I asked gently.

She looked up at me, her kind eyes narrowing slightly in curiosity. "Yes? Can I help you?"

"My name is Alasdair," I said, beads of sweat forming on my forehead. "I'm looking for Seraphine. Someone told me you might know where she is."

Mrs. Ellis studied me for a moment. Then she sighed, her shoulders slumping slightly. "Seraphine," she murmured, almost to herself. "That poor girl."

"Do you know where she went?"

She nodded slowly. "She said she's going back to where she came from."

"What do you mean? Her city?"

"Yes, dear. After two years of no contact with her family, she finally called her mother and told her about her heartbreak. Her mother asked her to come home. I think she's even considering getting engaged again. To her ex-fiancé." She said. The world around me came to a sudden halt.

Mrs. Ellis reached out and patted my hand. "If you care about her, don't waste time. She's been carrying a heavy burden, that one."

"I won't," I promised, already planning my trip in my mind.

"I've heard a lot about you. If she invites me and I get to know the address, I'll give it to you. You should go and get her." She smiled sympathetically.

I shook my head. "No... I won't go to get her back. I'd go to tell her the truth."

As I left the café, the weight in my chest grew. There was still a long road ahead, but it felt like I was moving toward her. And I wasn't going to stop until I found her. I had to tell her how much I loved her and why I did what I did. If she wants to get married to someone else, someone who doesn't say no after making her wait for eight years, I wouldn't mind. I'd rather be happy that she's with someone who can assure her a future. But before that, she needed to know my reason. She deserved to know.

## 28

# Alasdair

It was spring in Edinburgh, and the city seemed alive with renewal. The cherry blossoms along Princes Street swayed gently in the breeze, their petals falling like soft pink snow, carpeting the cobblestone paths below. The air was warming, carrying the faint scent of blooming flowers and freshly turned earth. The gardens and hills were bursting with colour, and the days were just long enough to let the light linger over the historic skyline.

I arrived in the city with a single purpose, but now, standing amidst the vibrant energy of spring, doubt crept in like a shadow. I had come here for her—to find Seraphine, to tell her the truth. But what if she was already building a life without me? What if spring, with all its promises of new beginnings, didn't have room for us anymore?

Mrs. Ellis had been kind enough to give me the address of the engagement hall, though part of me wondered if that was all it was—

a kindness, a way of sending me off without too much emotion. She had said Seraphine was looking for a new beginning, trying to put the past behind her. The thought of her starting over, with someone else, twisted in my stomach. But I had to see her, had to tell her the truth, even if it meant walking away from her for good afterward.

I hailed a cab, my mind racing as the driver took me through the city. The streets blurred past, the familiar cityscape mixing with memories of her: her laugh, her smile, the way she would lose herself in a book and forget the world around her.

The cab pulled up in front of the hall, a grand building adorned with white ribbons and flowers, the air alive with the chatter of people preparing for an event. I hesitated, unsure if I should go inside or wait for a sign. But then, I saw her.

Seraphine.

She was standing inside, speaking softly with a woman I didn't recognise, but her presence was unmistakable. She looked different, yet the same. Her hair was pulled back, her posture poised, but there was a certain weariness in her eyes that didn't go unnoticed. She wasn't the carefree, lost girl I had left behind. She was someone else now, someone I wasn't sure I could still reach.

I took a step forward, my heart hammering, but my feet felt rooted to the spot. I wasn't sure how to approach her, or what to say. The last time we had seen each other, everything had fallen apart.

But I couldn't walk away now.

With a deep breath, I crossed the threshold into the hall, the soft murmur of conversation growing louder as I made my way toward her. Seraphine turned as she heard the sound of my footsteps, her eyes widening in surprise.

"Alasdair?"

I stopped just a few feet from her, suddenly feeling small and exposed. "Seraphine," I said, my voice rough. "I—"

"What are you doing here?" She didn't let me finish.

"I came to find you," I said. "I needed to see you. To tell you everything. You deserve to know why I did that."

Her expression softened slightly, but there was still a distance between us, as if she was unsure if she should welcome me or shut me out.

Seraphine took a cautious step back, as though the space between us was both physical and emotional. She opened her mouth to speak, then closed it again, as if weighing her words carefully.

"I don't understand, Alasdair. Why?"

"I didn't mean to hurt you. I never wanted to make you feel like you were left behind, but I was scared. I didn't know how to explain what I was going through. I didn't know if you'd understand."

The woman, who I now recognised as Seraphine's mother, raised an eyebrow at me, her voice laced with a sharp, almost incredulous tone. "Who is this young man, Seraphine?" she asked, her eyes scanning me with a mix of curiosity and skepticism.

Seraphine froze for a moment, as if caught between two worlds—the one she had built here and the one I had come from. "Mom... he is—" She started, but before she could finish, her mother cut her off.

"Is he the ghost you were talking about?" she blurted, her hand flying to her mouth in an exaggerated gasp.

"Mom!" Seraphine's voice cracked, a mix of embarrassment and frustration evident in her eyes. Her face flushed a deep shade of red as she turned to me, her expression now a blend of apology and exasperation.

"I didn't mean to—" she began, but her mother was already shaking her head, narrowing her eyes with judgment.

"Why is he here, then? Hasn't making you lose years of your life been enough already?" Her mother's voice was biting, the anger in her words like a cold gust of wind.

Seraphine's hand shook as she reached out to gently take mine. "Mom, please. Let us have a talk," she said firmly. Without another word, she grabbed my arm and pulled me away, leading me toward a balcony on the second floor. The tension in the air followed us like a storm cloud, and I could feel her mother's gaze burning into my back.

The moment we stepped outside, the cool evening breeze hit us, and the sounds of the bustling event faded behind the thick, strained silence between us. Seraphine let go of my arm once we were safely out of earshot of her mother.

"I'm sorry about that," she said. Her voice was soft but edged with a kind of exhaustion. "My mom... she doesn't know everything. I didn't mean for you to be caught in the middle of that."

I shook my head. "It's fine. I just didn't expect the confrontation. Or for her to see me as a ghost."

Seraphine smiled faintly, but there was sadness in it. "It feels like that sometimes, doesn't it? Like you've come back from the dead after so long." She leaned against the balcony railing, staring out over the city. "When you left that day, I called her crying. She asked me to come back and start over where I left off. Not knowing what to do, I came back here."

"You could've waited a little. I know you've waited long enough. But getting engaged to someone who cheated on you? Isn't that a bit too harsh?"

"Then what should I have done, Alasdair? You love me, but you can't be with me. You love me, but you are still not ready to marry me. How can I wait for a man who doesn't see a future with me?"

"It's not that, Seraphine. It's just…"

"What is it?"

"I love you. More than myself. And that's why I can't have you."

"What do you mean? It makes no sense."

"The time I have does not have any guarantee. Today I'm here, tomorrow I may not be. How can I let the love of my life get involved with someone who has no assured future?"

"I don't understand." She came closer, her lips trembling. "What do you mean by no guarantee? Where are you going?" She grabbed me by my shoulders and breathed heavily as her eyes started glistening.

"Nowhere. Not yet."

"Yet? That means eventually you'll go?"

"I don't know. No one knows."

"Just tell me what's wrong with you. Will you?" She shook my shoulders.

"I've final stage peptic ulcer. Bleeding ulcer. It's quite serious and can be life-threatening."

"What?"

"Yes. I brought this upon myself. I stopped eating in the misery of thinking that I lost you forever. It's all my fault. That's why we can't be together. Good that you're getting engaged." A tear streaked down my cheek and I immediately wiped it with the back of my palm.

Seraphine stood still for a moment, her eyes wide with disbelief. She didn't speak at first, as though trying to process what I had just said. I could see the shock on her face, the confusion, the hurt. But above all, I saw something else—something softer. Concern.

"You—what?" She stepped closer, her voice trembling slightly. "Alasdair, why didn't you tell me this before? Why didn't you come to me?"

I looked away, unable to meet her eyes. "I didn't want you to see me like this. I didn't want to be the reason you couldn't move on. The reason you'd be tied to someone so broken, someone who couldn't even take care of himself."

Her hand reached for mine. Her touch was warm and grounding, just like how I felt when I first read her book. "That's not how I see you, Alasdair," she said gently, her fingers curling around mine. "You're not broken. And even if you were… you should have told me. We could have faced this together."

I let out a bitter laugh, shaking my head. "You don't understand, Seraphine. I thought I lost you forever. I thought you were gone from my life for good. And in that despair, I did this to myself. I shut myself off from everything, even my own health."

"You're not the only one who's suffered, Alasdair. You've been carrying this weight alone, but I've been carrying it too. We both have. And it doesn't have to be like that anymore. You don't have to do this alone."

"I didn't want to drag you back into my mess. After everything that happened, I thought it was better for you to just move on without me."

Seraphine shook her head slowly. "You think I could just forget you? That's not how love works. I never wanted to move on without you, Alasdair. I just had to try to survive without you. But now…" She paused, her eyes glistening with unshed tears. "Now I don't want to lose you again. Not like this."

A tear slipped down my cheek, and I quickly wiped it away, but Seraphine reached up and touched my face, her thumb gently brushing the trace of it. "Don't hide from me. Please. If there's even a chance, we can figure this out. Together."

"But what about your engagement? What about your future?" I asked, my voice faltering. "You deserve someone healthy, someone who can give you a real future."

"Maybe," she said softly, "but I've already chosen. I chose you, Alasdair. You're the one I've always wanted, the one I still want. If you'll let me."

Her words pierced me like nothing else. My heart ached, torn between the fear of hurting her and the desperate longing to have her back in my life. "I'm not asking for a fairy tale ending," I whispered. "I just want you to know why I did what I did. I never stopped loving you, Seraphine. And I never will."

She leaned in, her forehead resting against mine, her breath warm against my skin. "We'll figure this out," she whispered. "We'll find a way through it."

The world seemed to narrow around us, the noise of the crowd below fading into nothingness as I felt her breath on my lips. I could hear my heart pounding in my chest, louder than anything else. The warmth of her body so close, the gentle touch of her hands, everything pulled me toward her.

I closed my eyes, and without a word, I leaned in, hesitant at first, waiting for her to pull back, to tell me it was all too much. But she didn't. Instead, she closed the small distance between us, her lips brushing mine so softly, so tenderly, it felt like a dream.

The kiss deepened, and I lost myself in her—the years of separation, the pain, the doubt, all melted away. She tasted like the spring air outside, fresh and full of possibility. Her hands cupped my face, drawing me closer as if she never wanted to let go.

The kiss was everything—apology, yearning, love, and hope—all woven into a single, shared moment. Time seemed to stand still as I pulled her closer, our bodies pressed together, as though we were both trying to make up for lost time, for all the years apart.

When we finally pulled away, I could barely breathe. Her eyes were wide, and her cheeks took to the shade of the spring flowers. Neither of us spoke right away, the tranquility between us filled with everything we had just shared, everything we still had to say.

"I've waited for this for so long," she whispered against my lips.

"Me too," I breathed, my hand still gently holding hers. "But I'm not going to let go again. I promise."

And in that moment, I knew that whatever came next, whatever the future held, we would face it together.

## 29

# Alasdair

"Wait, what about your engagement? What will you do about it?" I asked, the question slipping out before I could stop myself.

Seraphine met my gaze, her expression serious but calm. "I'll call it off," she said with a serious voice. "I can't go through with it. Not when I know what's still between us."

"You're sure?" I asked, my voice a little shaky. "It's a huge step. You've already started a life with him…"

"I thought I could move on," she interrupted softly, her eyes never leaving mine. "But I was wrong. I thought marrying him would be a fresh start, a way to leave the past behind. But the truth is, I can't leave you behind. Not now, not ever."

"But… your family, your life here…" I trailed off, unsure of how to express what I was feeling.

"I'm not going to build a life based on a lie. I thought I could, but I can't. I can't live in a future that isn't real, and what we had—that's real. So, I'll call it off. I need to be honest with myself... and with you."

Her words, simple yet profound, sent a rush of emotions through me.

I took a deep breath, trying to steady my racing heart. "Are you sure? About everything? Because this changes everything. It's not just the engagement. It's everything."

"I've never been more sure of anything in my life. We both deserve the chance to see where this goes. Together." She replied.

"They say the world is small, but you made it infinite. Through your words, you became the map I never knew I was following." I said.

Seraphine's hand was warm in mine as we descended the stairs. I felt a mixture of anticipation and trepidation. The decision to call off the engagement was one thing, but confronting her mother? That was another.

Seraphine squeezed my hand, as though she sensed my hesitation. "It won't be easy," she murmured. "But I need her to understand. She deserves to know the truth, even if it's hard."

I nodded, my throat tight with unspoken words. I understood. This wasn't just about us anymore—it was about her family, the life she had tried to build, and the reality of what she was leaving behind.

We reached the bottom of the stairs, and I could see her mother talking quietly with a few guests near the front door. She was a striking woman, her features sharp and kind, but there was an unmistakable tension in the air around her. She turned as we approached, her gaze immediately landing on Seraphine before flicking to me.

"Seraphine," she began, her voice steady but with a hint of concern. "What is it? You've been gone for a while."

Seraphine took a deep breath, her gaze never wavering. "Mom, I need to talk to you. It's important."

"What is it?" Her mother's expression slowly started to shift to anger.

"I'm calling off the engagement!" Seraphine shouted. Our eyes almost fell out of the sockets. I didn't expect her to make a loud announcement.

"Seraphine! You didn't have to be so loud." I whispered, concern thickening my voice.

Everyone in the hall looked at us with their palms covering their mouth.

"Have you gone insane?" Her mother gasped.

"No. I finally feel sane."

"You're ending a true life for something that has been built on shaky ground. Asher is waiting for you, he was always waiting! Even when you ran away, he waited. How can you do this to him?"

Seraphine scoffed. "Of course, he was waiting. After all, his side chicks would never agree to marry him, I guess."

The entire hall fell silent, and her mother's gasp echoed in the heavy air. Guests began whispering among themselves, their shocked murmurs rippling like a wave through the crowd.

"Side chicks?" Her mother's voice cracked as she stared at Seraphine, disbelief written all over her face. "What are you talking about?"

Seraphine crossed her arms, her posture defiant. "I didn't want to air dirty laundry, but since we're here…" She glanced around at the audience, then back at her mother. "Asher isn't the saint everyone thinks he is. He was loyal until it was inconvenient for him. And you want me to spend my life with someone like that?"

"Seraphine, this isn't the place!" Her mother hissed, her cheeks flushed with embarrassment. "This is a public event. Do you even realise the consequences of what you're saying?"

"Consequences?" Seraphine scoffed, her tone sharp. "You mean the consequences of being honest? I've spent too long pretending, too long living for everyone else's expectations. If there are consequences for choosing my happiness, then so be it."

I wanted to speak, to step in and defend her, but I hesitated, unsure if it was my place. This was her battle, her truth to tell. Instead, I stayed by her side, my silent presence a show of support.

Her mother looked at me then, her eyes narrowing. "And this is your doing, isn't it?" she snapped. "You waltzed in here and filled her head with ideas of running away again, didn't you?"

"No," I said firmly, stepping forward. "This is all Seraphine. She's strong enough to make her own decisions, and I respect her for it. I didn't come here to take her away—I came to tell her the truth, to give her the choice."

"Choice?" Her mother's voice rose an octave. "This isn't about choice! This is about stability, about a future. What kind of future can you offer her?" Her words were cold, cutting through the air like a blade.

Seraphine turned to me, her expression a mix of anger and heartbreak. "You don't get to talk about him like that," she said, her voice trembling but strong. "He's the man I love. And he's worth more to me than any empty promise Asher could make."

Her mother opened her mouth to respond, but Seraphine cut her off. "I'm done living in fear of what people think, Mom. I'm calling off this engagement, again. And I'm doing it for me. Not for him, not for you. For myself."

The room seemed to hold its breath as her words hung in the air. Slowly, her mother's shoulders sagged, the fight draining from her. "You're sure about this?"

"I've never been more sure of anything," Seraphine replied.

Her mother looked at her for a long moment, then at me, before exhaling heavily. "Then I hope you know what you're doing," she said, turning away and walking toward the other end of the hall.

The tension in the room began to dissipate as Seraphine turned to me. "I did it," she whispered.

I reached for her hand, squeezing it gently. "You did. And I'm so proud of you."

As the guests slowly resumed their conversations, Seraphine and I stepped out of the hall, leaving the chaos behind.

## 30
## Alasdair

A week later, after all the dust had settled, we boarded a flight back to Inverness. Seraphine sat beside me, gazing out of the window as the world below dissolved into patchworks of green and brown.

Inverness wasn't just my hometown; it was the place I had buried myself in when I thought I'd lost her forever. The noiseless streets, the familiar stone buildings, the comfort of small cafes where no one asked questions—it had been my refuge. Now, it felt like it was waiting for a new chapter to begin.

"You know," Seraphine said, breaking the silence, her voice soft but steady, "I've always wanted to visit this part of Scotland. You used to write about it so vividly. I feel like I've been here a thousand times through your words."

I smiled, the corners of my mouth tugging upward as warmth spread through me. "Then you already know the best places to go," I replied. "Though I'll admit, it's even better in person. Did you discover any good place while you stayed here for two years?"

"No. I was so busy finding you that I failed to notice everything else." She turned to me, her eyes sparkling with curiosity. "Are you going to show me all of them?"

"Every single one," I promised.

The plane touched down, and as we stepped into the crisp, cool air of Inverness, I felt a strange sense of peace. I wasn't sure how everything would turn out—my health, our future—but for the first time in years, I wasn't scared. Seraphine was here, and that was enough for now.

We checked into a small, cozy inn on the edge of town, its ivy-covered stone walls radiating charm. As we unpacked, Seraphine pulled out her journal and settled into a chair by the window, the soft afternoon light casting a golden hue over her features.

"What are you writing?" I asked, leaning against the doorway.

She glanced up, her lips curving into a smile. "Just a few thoughts. Being here feels like the start of something... something I've been waiting for."

I walked over and knelt by her chair, taking her hand in mine. "That's because it is," I said softly. "This is our start, Seraphine. No more running, no more what-ifs. Just us."

She leaned down and kissed me, her lips warm and familiar, a reminder that we had fought through so much to get here. I felt like I was home—not because of the city, but because of her.

The days in Inverness passed in a haze of bliss and cautious hope. I showed Seraphine every corner of the city I had written about—the banks of the River Ness, where the water flowed calmly under ancient bridges; the grandeur of Inverness Castle perched high on a hill overlooking the city; and the little tea house tucked away on a silent street, where I had spent countless afternoons escaping my own thoughts.

The tea house was small and warm, with mismatched chairs and soft, worn rugs that muffled the sound of footsteps. The air was fragrant with the aroma of steeped herbs and freshly baked scones. Seraphine's eyes lit up the moment we walked in, her gaze flitting between the colourful jars of loose-leaf teas lining the shelves and the handwritten menu displayed on a chalkboard.

"This place is charming," she said, leaning closer to examine a tin labeled *Elderflower Dream*. "You really spent time here?"

I shrugged, smiling as I led her to a corner table by the window. "It's quiet, unassuming. The kind of place where no one asks too many questions. Perfect for getting lost in my own head."

She arched a brow, a playful smirk tugging at her lips. "You mean perfect for brooding?"

"Maybe," I admitted, unable to suppress a chuckle.

We ordered tea and shared a plate of pastries, talking as the golden afternoon light streamed through the window. Seraphine crumbled a piece of shortbread between her fingers as she spoke, her words coming easily in the intimate setting. "You know," she said, glancing around, "this place reminds me of that café I used to visit in Edinburgh when I was struggling to finish my second novel. Something about the hum of places like this makes it easier to think."

"Maybe it's the tea," I said lightly, taking a sip from my cup. "Calming. Grounding."

She smiled, her gaze lingering on mine. "Or maybe it's the company."

The air between us felt charged, full of unspoken words. The clink of teacups and the soft murmur of conversation faded into the background as I reached across the table to take her hand. Her fingers intertwined with mine, warm and steady.

The rain started to fall as we left the tea house, a soft drizzle that painted the cobblestones with a shimmering sheen. Seraphine glanced up at the sky, her hair catching faint droplets that gleamed like tiny jewels in the light. She smiled, tilting her face toward the rain as though welcoming it.

"You love the rain, don't you?" I asked, watching her with awe.

"I do," she replied, turning to me. "It feels… cleansing. Like it's washing away everything that doesn't matter and leaving only what's real."

I reached for her hand, the warmth of her fingers grounding me. "And what's real right now?" I asked, the question heavier than I intended.

She paused, looking down at our joined hands. "This," she said softly. "You. Us. Right here."

The vulnerability in her voice made my heart swell. I wanted to tell her how much this moment meant, how much she meant, but I couldn't form words. Instead, I laced my fingers through hers, holding on as if to tether myself to her.

"Come on," I said suddenly, a spark of mischief lighting in me. "Let's go."

"Go where?" she asked, laughing as I tugged her forward.

"Anywhere," I said, pulling her down the street as the rain began to fall harder. "Everywhere. Just... with you."

We ran through the streets of Inverness, the rain soaking through our clothes and making the world around us glisten with life. The air smelled of wet stone and blooming flowers, and the distant sound of the River Ness added a melody to our steps. Seraphine's laughter echoed through the streets, the sound filling the spaces in me I didn't realise had been empty.

We stopped beneath an old stone bridge, the arches providing a temporary shelter from the rain. Seraphine leaned against the cold stone, catching her breath, her cheeks flushed and her hair sticking to her face.

"You're mad," she said, though her grin betrayed her words.

"Maybe," I replied, stepping closer. "But you make me that way."

She looked up at me, her smile softening. "You know," she said. "I never thought I'd feel like this again. Like the world isn't so heavy."

I smiled to myself when I noticed that she said 'You know' a lot. It was like a part of her.

I reached out, brushing a damp strand of hair from her face. "You make the world feel lighter, Seraphine. You always have."

The space between us seemed to vanish, and before I knew it, our lips met. The kiss was soft at first, tentative, as though we were afraid to break the fragile moment. But then it deepened, and the world around us seemed to fade away.

When we finally pulled apart, her eyes searched mine, filled with hope and something I hadn't seen in years—peace.

"I'm scared," she admitted, her voice trembling. "But I don't want to let go of this. Of us."

"You won't have to," I promised, pulling her into my arms. "Not this time."

As the rain continued to fall, we stood there under the bridge, holding onto each other as though nothing else existed.

We walked through the streets of Inverness, the rain easing into a fine mist that clung to our hair and skin. Seraphine clung to my hand as we ventured beyond the city center, where the buildings gave way to open spaces and winding trails.

"I didn't think we'd end up out here," she said, glancing around. "What is this place?"

"It's a community garden," I said, leading her toward an old iron gate. "I come here sometimes when I need to clear my head. It's peaceful."

The gate creaked open, revealing rows of raised flower beds and winding stone paths. Even in the faint moonlight, the garden seemed alive, vibrant with the scent of lavender and fresh rain. Twinkling fairy lights hung from the trellises, their warm glow reflecting off drops of water clinging to the leaves.

"It's beautiful," Seraphine said, her voice hushed. She let go of my hand and wandered down one of the paths, her fingers grazing the petals of blooming wildflowers. I watched her as she explored, the way she seemed lighter, more at ease.

"This place feels like a secret," she said, turning back to me with a soft smile. "How did you find it?"

"A friend introduced me to it years ago," I said, walking toward her. "It's open to anyone, but it feels like it belongs to the people who really need it. I thought it might be the kind of place you'd like."

"You thought right," she said, her smile growing.

We wandered together through the garden, stopping occasionally to admire a particularly vibrant bloom or to simply take in the stillness of the night. The tension of the past few days seemed to melt away with every step, replaced by something steadier.

Eventually, we found a small bench tucked beneath an ivy-covered archway. We sat side by side, the world around us fading into the background.

"You always surprise me," she said, her head leaning against my shoulder.

"Good surprises or bad?" I teased, though my heart ached with how much I wanted to keep surprising her, to keep giving her moments like this.

"Always good," she replied.

The garden seemed to sing with life around us, the sound of distant raindrops and rustling leaves creating a melody that felt like it was just for us.

"I could stay here forever," she whispered.

I turned to her, the glow of the fairy lights catching in her eyes. "Then let's stay as long as we can," I said.

## 31
## Alasdair

The next day, we decided to take a bus trip to an amusement park far from Inverness. We boarded the bus early in the morning, excited for the adventure ahead. The long journey would give us plenty of time to talk and enjoy the scenery as we made our way through the Scottish countryside.

The bus was comfortable, and as it rolled down the winding roads, we passed through small towns and villages, the landscapes shifting from rolling hills to dense forests and expansive fields. We sat together, talking about everything and nothing, sharing stories of our childhoods and hopes for the future. There was something freeing about being on a bus—no rush, no expectations, just the open road ahead.

Seraphine smiled as we passed through a particularly scenic stretch of countryside. "This is so beautiful," she said, her voice soft and thoughtful. "It's like we're the only ones in the world right now."

I nodded, glancing out the window at the distant mountains and the endless green fields stretching out before us. "It feels like the whole world is in slow motion. Like time doesn't exist here."

After a few hours, we finally arrived at the amusement park. It was tucked away in a quiet part of the country, far from the bustle of city life. The park itself was a blend of old-fashioned charm and modern thrills, with towering roller coasters, colourful carnival rides, and game booths lining the walkways.

As we entered the park, the excitement in the air was contagious. The smell of cotton candy and popcorn mixed with the sound of laughter and cheerful music. We walked hand in hand, taking it all in, knowing that this day—just us, the rides, and the thrill of the moment—was exactly what we needed.

"I can't remember the last time I felt this carefree," Seraphine said, grinning as we passed a bumper car ride.

"Let's make sure we don't forget," I replied, my heart lighter than it had been in a long time. There was something about the simple joy of being here, away from the pressures and complications of life, that made everything feel possible again.

We made our way to the roller coaster, the towering metal structure casting a long shadow over the park. Seraphine's eyes sparkled with excitement as she tugged me toward the line.

"This one looks amazing!" she exclaimed, her face lighting up.

I hesitated, but she was already pulling me toward the seats. The last thing I wanted was to ruin her fun, so I pushed my worries to the back of my mind and climbed into the ride. As we strapped ourselves in, the rush of anticipation filled the air, and I couldn't help but feel a twinge of excitement despite myself.

The roller coaster began its slow climb, and I could feel my heart beating in sync with the rising track. The view from the top was breathtaking—the entire park stretched out beneath us, and the distant hills looked like a painting under the golden light of the afternoon. But as the coaster tipped over the edge and plummeted down into a dizzying drop, I felt something shift inside me.

The twists and turns sent my stomach spinning in ways I hadn't prepared for. I tried to keep my eyes open, to stay in the moment with Seraphine, but the nausea hit me hard. My head spun, and a cold sweat broke out across my forehead. As we zoomed through loop-de-loops and sharp turns, I felt the world around me start to close in.

By the time the ride ended and the coaster came to a stop, I was struggling to keep my balance. My vision was blurry, my stomach churned uncontrollably, and the sense of unease that had been creeping up on me suddenly became overwhelming.

"Are you okay?" Seraphine's voice sounded distant, as though I were underwater. I turned to look at her, but my stomach lurched again.

Before I could respond, the wave of nausea became too much. I stumbled away from the seat, barely making it off the ride before I retched violently. The moment I threw up, I felt a sharp, burning pain in my chest. And then, to my horror, I saw the blood. Dark and thick, mixed with the vomit, it spread across the pavement.

"Alasdair!" Seraphine's voice pierced through the panic in my mind. I heard her feet pounding toward me and felt her arms catch me just as my legs buckled beneath me.

"Are you okay? What's happening? Oh my god, there's blood!" Her voice trembled with fear as she tried to support me. "We need to get you to a hospital, right now."

I tried to wave her off, but my body felt heavy, and my vision started to fade. "I… I'm fine… Just a little sick, it's nothing…" I muttered, though the words felt hollow, the reality of the situation settling in around me.

"Stop! Stop saying that!" She almost shouted, holding onto me tighter. "You're not fine. Please, Alasdair, don't do this. Please don't leave me again." Her voice cracked, and I could hear the panic building.

"I'm sorry," I whispered, the guilt and fear rushing in. The pain in my chest intensified, and I knew something was terribly wrong. "I didn't want this to happen…"

"I'm taking you to the hospital, now," she said firmly, her voice laced with both determination and fear. She pulled me toward the entrance of the park, her steps fast and frantic as she tried to keep me on my feet.

Every part of me wanted to reassure her, to tell her everything was fine, but the blood, the pain, the exhaustion—they made it impossible to pretend anymore. I had to face the truth.

Seraphine's grip on my arm tightened as she rushed me through the park, the sound of our hurried footsteps echoing in the chaotic noise of the amusement park. I could feel her anxiety rising with each passing second, and I hated that I was the cause of it.

"Hold on, Alasdair," she pleaded, her voice cracking as we pushed through the gates of the park. "We're almost there. Just stay with me, okay? Stay with me."

I nodded weakly, but the world felt distant. My chest burned, my head swam, and the sensation of blood in my throat was enough to make me dizzy. I tried to focus on her words, on the warmth of her hand, but the pain in my body was louder than anything else.

The bus station was a few hundred meters away, and we made it there in what felt like forever. Seraphine flagged down a taxi, practically throwing herself into the backseat with me as we both gasped for breath. She quickly gave the driver the address to the nearest hospital, and he immediately sped off.

I leaned my head against the window, trying to keep my breathing steady, but everything felt so wrong. I could feel Seraphine's gaze on me, her worry so palpable that it made me feel even worse. I wanted to reassure her, tell her it wasn't as bad as it seemed, but I couldn't find the words. The truth was too harsh, too final.

The ride to the hospital felt endless, though it was only a few minutes. By the time we arrived, I was barely able to stand on my own. Seraphine helped me out of the car, her arms steadying me as she rushed me inside, shouting for help.

The nurses were quick to react, taking one look at me before moving into action. They wheeled me into a treatment room, and I could hear their voices as they began working. I heard Seraphine's frantic voice asking questions, but I couldn't focus enough to understand what she was saying. All I could feel was the pressure in my chest, the weakness in my limbs, and the deep, unsettling fear that something was wrong.

As the doctor entered the room, I finally caught a glimpse of Seraphine's face. She looked pale, her eyes wide with fear as she looked between me and the medical staff.

The doctor didn't waste time with pleasantries. "We need to get him stabilized," he said firmly, and I felt a sharp sting in my arm as he administered an IV.

I turned to Seraphine, my voice barely above a whisper. "I'm sorry," I managed. "I didn't want this... I didn't want to hurt you."

Her eyes softened, though the worry never left her face. She stepped closer to the bed, her hand gently brushing my forehead. "You didn't hurt me, Alasdair," she said quietly. "You've never hurt me. But you have to fight. Please, don't leave me now."

I wanted to tell her that I would fight, that I would get through this somehow, but I couldn't. I could feel the darkness creeping in, the sense of uncertainty hanging heavy over everything. But I wasn't ready to let go—not now, not after everything we'd been through.

"Please," I whispered again. "I need you."

Her hand tightened around mine, and she leaned in, her forehead resting against mine. "I'm here, Alasdair," she said, her voice a soft promise. "I'm not going anywhere."

The steady beep of the heart monitor was the only sound in the room, its rhythm growing louder in my ears as I lay there, struggling to stay awake. The pain in my stomach hadn't subsided, but Seraphine's presence kept me tethered to the world, a fragile lifeline in the fog that threatened to swallow me.

I felt her hand still holding mine, warm and steady. Every so often, I felt her brush her thumb over my knuckles, a small but constant reassurance that she was there. I turned my head slightly, just enough to catch a glimpse of her. Her face was pale, her eyes red from the worry she couldn't hide, but there was a softness in her expression, a tenderness that cut through the chaos of the moment.

"I'm sorry, Seraphine," I whispered again, the words choking me. I wanted to say more, to explain everything I had failed to say before, but it felt impossible.

She squeezed my hand, shaking her head gently. "No need to apologize," she said softly, her voice still strained. "You don't have to explain anything right now. Just focus on getting better. I'm not going anywhere."

I closed my eyes briefly, fighting the dizziness that threatened to overtake me. Her words felt like a balm to my soul, the steady anchor I needed in a sea of uncertainty. But even as I clung to that, a deep fear lingered in the back of my mind—what if I wasn't going to be okay?

The doctor entered the room a few moments later, his expression serious but not overly alarmed. He glanced at the IV, checking the drip, before turning his attention to me.

"How are we feeling?" he asked.

"Not great," I rasped. "But… I think I'm okay."

The doctor raised an eyebrow, clearly not convinced. "You've lost quite a bit of blood," he said. "It's good you got here when you did, but we'll need to monitor you closely over the next few hours. We'll do some tests to make sure there's no further damage. The ulcer is severe, and we need to keep an eye on your condition."

I nodded weakly, my mind foggy but trying to process his words. It was like I was hearing them through a thick veil, the details fading in and out as my body seemed to shut down around me.

"Is there anything we should be concerned about right now?" Seraphine asked, her voice sharp with concern.

The doctor looked at her, then back at me. "We just need to keep him stable for the moment," he said. "He'll likely need more blood work, possibly a transfusion, depending on how his levels respond. The ulcer's bleeding has slowed for now, but it could worsen again. We'll be keeping a close watch."

I caught Seraphine's gaze, her worry etched on every line of her face. She didn't speak, but I could see her mind racing with a thousand questions.

The doctor finished his assessment, offering a few final instructions before he left the room, leaving us alone again. Seraphine stayed close, her hand never leaving mine.

"I... I don't know what's going to happen. I don't know if I'll make it."

"Stop. Don't think that way. You're going to be okay. I'm not leaving you. We'll get through this."

Tears welled up in my eyes, threatening to spill over, but I blinked them away. The pain in my chest, the fear, all of it felt so overwhelming.

Soon, my phone started to ring. It was Albert.

"How have you been?" he asked, his voice carrying a sense of concern that was rare for him.

"I'm at the hospital," I replied, the words sounding strange even to me as I said them.

"What? What happened?" His tone sharpened instantly, worry edging his voice.

"It's the ulcer… it got worse. I… I passed out at the park, and the bleeding started again," I explained, my voice weak. I didn't want to go into all the details, but Albert deserved to know.

"Shit, man. Are you okay?"

"I'll be fine. They're keeping an eye on me." I didn't want to sound reassuring, but I needed to believe it. The fear still lingered in the pit of my stomach.

Albert paused, and I could hear him moving around on the other end. "I'll be there as soon as I can," he said. "You're not in this alone, okay?"

I smiled softly despite the pain. "I know. Thanks, Albert."

"Don't thank me yet. Just hang in there. You'll pull through."

"Yeah," I muttered, feeling a little more comforted by his words. "I'll try."

The line went silent for a moment as I heard the faint rustle of the hospital room door. I turned my head slightly, catching Seraphine's eyes. Her gaze was full of concern, but there was an underlying strength in her presence that I needed now more than ever.

"I'll let you know if anything changes," I said, my voice steadying as I spoke to Albert. "Talk to you soon."

"Take care of yourself, Alasdair," he said before hanging up.

I lowered the phone. Seraphine shifted closer, brushing her fingers against my hand.

"Who was that?" she asked softly.

"Albert, my friend," I replied, my gaze meeting hers. "He's on his way."

"Good," she said, nodding, though her face was still etched with worry. "You're not going through this alone."

I nodded, trying to believe her. But there was still a part of me that couldn't shake the fear—the uncertainty that loomed ahead. Even if I was surrounded by people who cared about me, even if I wasn't alone in this moment, the future still felt fragile.

Will I survive, or will I fade into the silence, lost to the shadows of time? I don't know.

## 32

# Alasdair

The morning after began with new beginnings, both positive and negative. I woke up with Seraphine staring at my face while holding my hand close to her chest. A soft knock at the door broke the silence. Dr. Fraser entered, his expression calm but serious, a clipboard in his hand. Seraphine straightened in her chair, tightening her grip.

"Good morning, Alasdair," the doctor began, glancing between the two of us. "I have the results of your tests."

My stomach churned as I nodded. "Go on, Doc."

Dr. Fraser took a measured breath. "The ulcer in your stomach is quite severe. The bleeding has caused significant damage to the surrounding tissue. Left untreated, it could result in perforation or life-threatening complications."

Seraphine's hand trembled in mine. "What does this mean for him?" she asked.

"It means we need to act immediately," Dr. Fraser replied in a steady but grave tone. "We'll have to perform surgery to remove the ulcer and repair the damaged area. It's a major operation, and the recovery will take time. But without it, the risks are too great."

"What's the success rate?" I asked.

"The procedure itself is generally safe," Dr. Fraser said, meeting my gaze directly. "But given the extent of the damage and your current condition, the road ahead won't be easy. You'll need to make significant lifestyle changes and commit to a rigorous recovery process."

I nodded numbly, the words swirling in my mind. Seraphine leaned closer, her other hand brushing my cheek and her eyes brimming with tears. "You hear that?" she whispered. "You can do this. We'll get through this."

"Seraphine, you don't have to—"

"Don't you dare finish that sentence," she interrupted, her voice fierce despite the tears streaking her face. "I'm not going anywhere, Alasdair. You're stuck with me, no matter how hard this gets."

Her words broke something inside me, and I pulled her into a tight embrace, burying my face in her shoulder. "I don't know if I can do this," I murmured.

"Yes, you can," she said firmly. "And you're not doing it alone."

Dr. Fraser gave us a moment before speaking again. "I'll leave you two to process this. A nurse will come by to discuss the next steps and prepare you for surgery. You're in good hands, Alasdair."

The hours that followed were a haze of preparations, paperwork, and medical explanations. The nurses came and went with warm smiles and reassurance.

As evening fell, a nurse entered to administer the pre-surgery routine, giving instructions on fasting and preparation. Seraphine helped me settle into the hospital bed, fluffing the pillows and arranging the thin blanket over me.

"You know," she said lightly. "this is just another adventure we'll laugh about someday."

"I guess I've always had a flair for the dramatic."

She chuckled softly, sitting down beside me and taking my hand. "Promise me one thing, Alasdair."

"Anything," I said without hesitation.

"When this is over, we'll make a list of all the things we want to do together. And we'll do them. No more holding back, no more waiting. Life's too unpredictable for that."

"I promise," I said. "We'll do everything on that list. Starting with... I don't know, maybe going on a trip where I don't end up in a hospital?"

She laughed. "Deal."

When the nurse finally returned to let me know it was time to sleep, Seraphine leaned in, her forehead resting gently against mine. "I'll be right here when you wake up."

The day of the surgery arrived, and it felt like the world had slowed down to a crawl. I lay in the hospital bed, the sterile white sheets tucked around me as the sound of machines filled the otherwise silent room. There was no turning back now—today, everything would change, for better or worse.

The sun barely peeped through the small window, casting long shadows across the room, making it feel colder than it actually was. I tried to focus on my breathing, and on calming my mind, but the anxiety was impossible to shake off. A million thoughts rushed through my head—about what could go wrong, what might happen after.

My love sat by my side, her hand resting on mine, her fingers tracing small circles on my palm. She hadn't said much, but she didn't need to. Her support spoke volumes.

"Are you sure you want to go through with this?" she asked softly, breaking the stillness. Her voice was gentle, yet there was an underlying urgency in her words.

I turned to face her, offering the most reassuring smile I could muster. "I don't really have a choice, do I?"

Her lips pressed into a thin line, but she nodded. "Just know I'm here."

I squeezed her hand, trying to convey everything I couldn't say. My heart raced, but it wasn't just fear—it was the overwhelming gratitude I felt for her. At this moment, with the surgery ahead and the uncertainty of the future hanging in the air, she was the only thing that felt certain.

The door opened, and the surgeon stepped in. "It's time," he said, offering me a reassuring smile.

I glanced at Seraphine one last time, my heart heavy with emotions I couldn't put into words. "I'll see you soon," I whispered, though I wasn't sure if I believed it.

She gave me a small, reassuring nod. "I'll be waiting, Alasdair."

As the nurses prepared me for the surgery, I tried to focus on that—her words, her promise. It was the one thing I could hold on to, the one thing that mattered.

## 33

# Seraphine

The fluorescent lights in the hallway flickered above, but all I could focus on was Alasdair—his pale face, the slight tremor in his hand as they wheeled him away. My heart felt like it was beating in double-time, racing against the tide of panic that was rising within me.

The surgical team moved quickly, their faces masked with professional efficiency, but I couldn't bring myself to look at any of them. I could only look at him.

"Alasdair," I whispered as I took a step closer, m. For a moment, I thought he might wake up, might say something to reassure me. But the sedation had already kicked in, and he lay there, so still, so vulnerable.

I had promised him we'd face this together, that we'd never walk away from each other. Yet, as the door to the operating room loomed ahead, I felt the terrifying weight of my words. What if I failed him? What if this was the moment everything slipped through my fingers?

"Don't be scared," I whispered, my words more for myself than for him. "You're going to be fine. I won't let anything happen to you."

The nurse guiding the bed nodded, and I hesitated, wanting to stay by his side, but knowing I couldn't. I couldn't follow him in there. I couldn't stand there while they took him apart, trying to fix what had broken inside of him.

The walls of this sterile, cold hospital felt suffocating. Everything around me was moving at a pace I couldn't keep up with, and I was left standing still, holding on to the fading image of his face as he was taken farther and farther away from me.

"Seraphine," I heard a voice—someone, probably a nurse—calling my name, snapping me out of my daze. "You need to wait here, okay? They'll update you as soon as they can."

I nodded, not trusting myself to speak, and my eyes stayed locked on the door as they wheeled him through it. My hands trembled as I clasped them together, trying to steady myself, to hold it together.

What if something went wrong? What if this was the last time I'd see him awake? The questions screamed in my mind, but I couldn't answer any of them. All I could do was wait.

I turned, taking a seat in the nearest chair, my hands still shaking. I wanted to scream, to demand that they fix him, that they make everything better. But I knew, deep down, that there was nothing I could do but trust in the doctors, and Alasdair's strength.

"Please come back to me."

And I waited. I waited for the man I loved to return, for the surgery to end, for the world to feel whole again.

The soft shuffle of footsteps, the distant murmur of voices—they all blended into a dull, suffocating soundtrack to my thoughts. Each second that passed felt like another weight on my chest, pressing harder, suffocating me.

I tried to focus on the waiting room, tried to focus on the soft chairs, and the calming decor, but my mind was consumed by him.

I kept replaying the moments before the surgery. I had tried to reassure him, but deep down, I wasn't sure if I was reassuring him or myself.

I felt the tears welling in my eyes again, but I fought them back, refusing to give in to fear. I couldn't break down. Not yet. Not while he was still out there, fighting for his life.

The door to the waiting room opened, and a nurse stepped inside. I jumped to my feet, my heart leaping in my chest.

"Is he okay?" I asked, my voice trembling despite my best efforts to keep it steady.

The nurse gave me a small, professional smile. "They've completed the surgery. It went well, but it'll take some time before he wakes up. He's stable for now."

I exhaled sharply, feeling like I could finally breathe again, even if it was just for a moment. Stable. That was a word I could hold on to.

"Can I see him?" I asked, already standing, my legs almost forgetting how to move as I tried to make my way toward her.

She nodded. "He's in recovery. You can see him shortly, once he's settled. Just give us a little more time."

I nodded, her words offering a temporary comfort. "Thank you."

I sank back into my seat, a fresh wave of exhaustion washing over me. I wanted to go to him. I wanted to be by his side when he woke up, to hold his hand and remind him that he wasn't alone.

But for now, I had to wait.

It felt like the longest wait of my life. Time seemed to crawl as I sat there, my mind alternating between anxious thoughts and memories of Alasdair—his smile, his warmth, the way he always seemed to know exactly what I needed, even when I didn't. I could still hear his voice in my head, his calm, reassuring tone. I held on to it like a lifeline.

Then, just as I thought I might go mad with the waiting, the nurse returned.

"He's awake now," she said. "You can see him."

I didn't wait for her to finish the sentence. I was already standing, already moving.

"Thank you," I whispered, my voice full of emotion.

The nurse led me down the long corridor, and my heart raced as we neared the recovery room. Every step felt like the beat of a song I couldn't wait to hear again. I stopped at the door, peeking inside. There he was, lying in the bed, eyes closed, a slight furrow between his brows.

I stepped into the room, the beeping of the machines surrounding us. Slowly, I walked to his bedside and gently took his hand, relief flooding me as his fingers twitched at my touch.

"Alasdair," I whispered. "I'm here. You made it."

His eyes fluttered open, and for a moment, he didn't seem to recognise where he was. But then, his eyes met mine, and the sweetest smile curved on his lips.

"Seraphine," his voice was hoarse. "You're here."

"I'm here," I said, squeezing his hand tighter. "I'm not going anywhere. Not now, not ever."

His eyes softened, and I saw the gratitude in them—just as much as the exhaustion. I leaned down, brushing my lips against his forehead, feeling his warmth, his heartbeat beneath my fingers.

"I love you."

"I love you too."

A few days later, Alasdair was finally discharged from the hospital. The doctor had given him a clean bill of health, saying that he needed rest and a little time to fully recover, but that his surgery had gone well. Though he was weak, the relief in his eyes was enough to make me smile, knowing that we had crossed the hardest part of this journey.

Alasdair and I left the hospital together, walking slowly. When we arrived at the apartment, I could feel the tension in the air. Albert had already been packing up his things, giving us space as we transitioned into our new life. I wasn't sure what I expected, but I had been so caught up in the whirlwind of everything, I hadn't truly considered what this would mean for Albert.

"I'll be gone by the end of the day," he said. "I think it's better this way. You both need time to heal, to figure things out."

I could see the mixture of emotions on his face. There was no animosity, no bitterness. Just understanding.

"Thanks, Albert," Alasdair said, his voice rough from the few days of being in and out of consciousness. "You've been a good friend. I'm sorry for everything. I know this was hard."

Albert shook his head, smiling ever so softly. "There's nothing to apologise for. You're both in a better place now. That's all that matters."

It was a bittersweet moment, but it felt like the right thing for all of us. With a final nod, Albert grabbed the last of his things and headed out the door, leaving us standing there, alone.

I looked at Alasdair, who was still a little pale. He had been through so much, and I couldn't help but marvel at how he was still standing here beside me.

"Are you okay?" I asked, walking over to him.

"I will be. With you, I will be."

## 34

# Seraphine

"Hey," I said, flipping through a notebook. "Do you ever think about all the things we never did?"

Alasdair looked at me, his lips curving into a small smile. "Like what?"

I shrugged. "Just… little things. Simple things we never got around to."

He raised an eyebrow. "Like what kind of things?"

I grabbed a pen. "How about a picnic? Just us, a blanket, and sandwiches in the park?"

He chuckled, nodding. "I'm in."

He grabbed the pen from me. "I've always wanted to cook something complicated, like homemade pasta."

I laughed. "You can try, but I'm making sure the fire extinguisher is nearby."

We both laughed, adding more ideas to the list: stargazing, movie marathons, weekend getaways. Each one felt like a small promise.

"Do you think we'll get through all of it?" he asked.

I smiled. "Doesn't matter. It's about doing it together."

"Yeah," he agreed softly. "Together."

As we continued to jot down more ideas, the room felt warmer, more cozy, even though the outside world seemed distant. Every little suggestion we made felt like a piece of the future we could finally start building.

"I was thinking," I said, tapping the pen against the page, "maybe we could take a painting class together. You know, get messy with the colours and forget what we're supposed to be doing."

Alasdair looked at me, his eyes lighting up with amusement. "I can already picture you covered in paint, looking like a masterpiece gone wrong."

"Hey," I said, grinning, "I'd be a work of art."

He chuckled, leaning back against the couch. "Alright, it's on the list. But I'm warning you, I'm no Picasso."

"Doesn't matter," I replied. "It's about the fun, not the outcome."

He nodded, smiling softly. "We could do this forever, couldn't we? Just... trying new things together."

I nodded, feeling my heart settle into a peaceful rhythm. "I think that's the best part. We're still figuring it all out, but we're doing it together."

## 35
## Seraphine

We spent the next three years ticking off the list of things we'd once dreamed of doing together. Every weekend was an adventure—a picnic in the park, a trip to the coast, or a hike through the hills, our hands always intertwined. We laughed over cooking classes, tried new hobbies we'd never thought of before, and spent lazy afternoons in bookstores and cafés, savouring the simplicity of being with each other.

The list we made was no longer just a list; it became our shared journey, full of memories that stitched us even closer. From spontaneous road trips to quiet evenings at home, we made every moment count.

One fine evening, as the soft glow of the setting sun filled our living room, I turned to him, curiosity in my voice. "What made you keep waiting, even when I disappeared without a word?"

He paused, his gaze drifting toward the window for a moment as if gathering the right words from the space between us. Then, with a soft smile, he answered, "Where ink hesitates, and silence takes form, the heart's truest confessions begin."

The room was quiet except for the soft crackle of the fire, its amber light dancing across the walls. The evening had a kind of stillness to it, the kind where even time seemed to slow as if the universe were holding its breath. He shifted beside me on the couch, his movements deliberate yet hesitant, as if he were carrying a secret too fragile to speak aloud.

"Seraphine," he said, breaking the silence. "Will you forever let me be your poet?"

I blinked, unsure if I had heard him correctly, but the look in his eyes left no room for doubt.

Before I could respond, he reached into his pocket and pulled out a small box. I gasped as he opened it to reveal a delicate ring. The design was simple but perfect—a single stone framed by a band that twisted like vines, intricate yet unassuming, like the beauty of a handwritten poem.

"I've written countless words for you. About you, for you, even in the moments when I thought you were lost to me. But none of them could ever capture how much you mean to me. You've been my muse, my hope, my reason to keep going when I thought I couldn't. And now, I don't want to just write about you—I want to build a life with you. A story. A home. I don't want another day to pass without you knowing that every line I write, every thought I have, will always lead back to you."

Tears started to form in my eyes, blurring the ring, his face, the firelight—but not his words. They settled into my chest, warm and weighty, like an anchor holding me steady. I didn't know I was crying until he reached up to gently brush a tear from my cheek.

"Sera," he whispered, "will you let me stay by your side, not just for now, but for always?"

I couldn't speak for a moment. I nodded, a shaky laugh breaking free as I wiped at my tears.

"Yes," I finally managed. "Yes, I'll let you be my poet. Always. Forever."

"This is the start of something I'll never stop writing, Seraphine. You and me."

The days that followed felt like they were plucked from the pages of a storybook. Every moment was infused with a new kind of joy that we were building something unshakable together.

We threw ourselves into planning not just a wedding, but a future that reflected every piece of who we were. It wasn't about extravagance or tradition—it was about us. Long walks along the river turned into conversations about where we'd live, what kind of adventures we'd chase, and how we'd make time for the little things that mattered most.

One afternoon, as the rain pattered gently against the windows, Alasdair sat at his desk, pen in hand, a look of focus on his face. I leaned against the doorway, watching him write, his brow furrowed slightly in concentration.

"You're writing again," I said softly, stepping into the room.

He glanced up, his expression easing into a smile. "For you, always."

I moved closer, tilting my head to see the paper. "What's this one about?"

"It's about promises," he said, a hint of shyness in his voice. "About the way love can rewrite you, even when you think the ink has run dry."

I sat beside him, resting my chin on his shoulder as I read the words he'd crafted. They weren't just poetry—they were pieces of him, etched onto the page with a kind of vulnerability that took my breath away.

When I looked at him, his eyes met mine with the same unwavering intensity I'd felt the night he proposed. "Do you know what you've done to me?" he asked.

"What have I done?" I teased, though my heart quickened at his tone.

"You've turned my words into a home," he whispered. "And I never want to leave it."

I kissed him then, a soft kiss that said everything I couldn't put into words.

Our days were filled with more than just planning. We danced in the kitchen to old records, got lost in bookstores hunting for treasures, and sat in the park, making lists of dreams we'd chase together.

On one of those evenings, under a sky scattered with stars, Alasdair turned to me, his fingers entwined with mine.

"This," he said, his voice filled with wonder. "This is the life I was waiting for. With you."

I smiled, leaning into him, my heart full. "And it's only just beginning."

It wasn't about perfect days or grand gestures. It was about us—two people who had weathered storms and found their way back to each other, ready to write the next chapter, hand in hand.

## 36

# Seraphine

I woke up to the sound of rain gently tapping against the window. For a moment, I thought it was just another peaceful morning in Inverness. But then the excitement surged through me like lightning.

I turned to my side, where Alasdair lay sound asleep, his face softened in the dim light of early dawn. How could he sleep so soundly today? Today!

I bit my lip to stifle my giddiness, but it was no use. "Alasdair," I whispered, leaning closer to him. No response.

"Alasdair!" I shook his shoulder lightly, my voice just a little louder.

His eyes fluttered open, and he groaned softly. "What is it, Sera? What time is it?"

"It's 5 a.m.," I said, barely able to contain my grin.

He blinked at me, his brow furrowing. "5 a.m.?" he repeated incredulously. "Why are you awake?"

"Because it's our wedding day!" I couldn't help the laugh that escaped me.

He let out a groggy chuckle, rubbing his face with one hand. "Of course. And you couldn't wait a few more hours to tell me that?"

"Absolutely not," I said, crossing my arms in mock indignation. "How can you be so calm?"

He propped himself up on one elbow, his smile growing. "Because I already know that by the end of the day, you'll be my wife. Why would I worry about anything else?"

His words hit me like a soft melody, and I felt my cheeks flush. How did he always know exactly what to say to calm me?

"Well," I said, climbing out of bed, "if you're not worried, then at least pretend to be excited. We have a lot to do!"

He reached for my hand as I started to move away, pulling me back toward him. "Seraphine," he said, his voice softer now. "I'm more than excited. I just like to keep it all here." He tapped his chest with his free hand, his eyes locked with mine.

My heart melted. "Good," I whispered, leaning down to kiss his forehead. "Because today is going to be perfect."

And with that, I pulled him out of bed, ready to begin the best day of our lives.

The day unfolded in a flurry of preparations, laughter, and tender moments. By mid-morning, the house was bustling with energy. My closest friends were there to help me get ready, their cheerful chatter filling the air. The scent of freshly brewed tea mingled with the soft floral notes from the bouquets delivered earlier.

I sat by the window, a pale beam of sunlight streaming through the curtains, as the makeup artist worked her magic. My wedding dress hung on the door—a delicate creation of lace and silk that felt like a dream come to life. I couldn't stop glancing at it, my heart racing every time I thought about walking down the aisle to Alasdair.

My thoughts were interrupted by a knock at the door. "Seraphine?"

It was Albert's voice.

"Come in!" I called, smiling as he entered.

He looked dapper in his suit, his expression warm as he took in the scene. "You look beautiful already," he said, then hesitated. "And nervous."

I laughed softly. "Is it that obvious?"

He nodded, walking over to sit beside me. "It's a big day. But you're going to be fine. You and Alasdair? You're written in the stars."

His words steadied me, and I reached out to squeeze his hand. "Thank you, Albert. For everything."

Downstairs, I heard a commotion—likely Alasdair getting teased by his friends or struggling with his tie. The thought made me smile.

Soon, it was time. My dress fit perfectly, its soft train whispering against the floor as I walked out of the room. My hair was pinned in soft waves, a subtle veil cascading down my back. Everyone stopped to stare as I descended the staircase, their faces lighting up with admiration.

"You're breathtaking," Albert said, his voice full of pride.

The ceremony was being held at a small stone chapel surrounded by fields of heather and wildflowers. The sky was a clear, endless blue, as though nature herself had blessed the day.

As the car pulled up, I saw Alasdair standing at the altar through the open doors. He looked nervous, fidgeting with his cufflinks, but when our eyes met, his expression softened into something that made my knees weak.

The music began, and everything else melted away.

Each step down the aisle brought me closer to him, to the life we had fought so hard to build. When I finally reached him, his hands trembled slightly as he took mine.

"You look—" he began, but his voice caught.

"You too," I whispered, my smile breaking through the tears already welling up in my eyes.

The ceremony was simple but heartfelt. When it came time for the vows, Alasdair surprised me with his.

"I used to think love was just a story written by others. But then you came into my life, Seraphine. You turned my silences into poetry, my doubts into dreams. I vow to be your poet forever, to write our story in every moment we share."

When it was my turn, I held his hands softly, my voice shaking. "Alasdair, you are the song I never knew my heart was waiting to hear. You are my home, my safe place. I vow to be your poem forever, to love you through every verse, even after the last word."

The kiss that sealed our vows felt like the culmination of everything we had been through. It was soft, tender, and filled with a love so profound it made the world around us disappear.

As we walked out of the chapel, hand in hand, the cheers of our friends and family ringing in our ears, I knew that this was just the beginning. The rest of our lives appeared before our eyes, a story waiting to be written. And we would write it together.

## 37
## Seraphine

The reception was nothing short of magical. The sun was setting as everyone moved into the outdoor marquee draped with fairy lights and decorated with wildflowers. The soft golden glow created an ambiance that felt intimate and enchanting. Friends and family mingled, laughter and joy filling the air as glasses clinked and plates were piled high with the delicious spread prepared for the evening.

Alasdair and I sat at the centre table, surrounded by those who loved us most. The speeches were heartfelt and often humorous, each one a reminder of how far we had come and how much support we had from the people around us. Albert's toast brought the crowd to tears, and his teasing about our stubborn love earned him a round of applause.

"You better treat her like royalty, Alasdair," he said, raising his glass. "Because if you don't, she's got an entire army of us to remind you."

Alasdair grinned and nodded, his hand firmly holding mine. "She's the queen of my heart, Albert. Always."

The evening rolled on, and soon the dance floor was alive with movement. Alasdair and I shared our first dance as husband and wife, swaying to a song that had always felt like ours.

"Still nervous?" he asked softly.

"Not anymore," I whispered. "Not when I'm with you."

As the night wore on, the music picked up, and everyone joined the dance floor. The energy was infectious, and we laughed until our cheeks ached. But somewhere around dessert, I noticed Alasdair's face had grown pale.

"Are you okay?" I asked, leaning in to touch his arm.

He winced slightly, placing a hand over his stomach. "I think it's just the food," he said with a small smile, trying to reassure me. "Maybe I overdid it with the appetisers."

"Do you need a break?" I asked, concern lacing my voice.

"No, I'm fine," he insisted, but as the minutes passed, his discomfort became more apparent.

Finally, after a whispered conversation, we decided to wrap up the reception early. I made an announcement, thanking everyone for coming and asking them to continue celebrating in their own way as we quietly slipped away.

Back at the house, I helped Alasdair out of his jacket and loosened his tie as he sat down on the couch. "Maybe it's just the rich food," I said, trying to keep my voice calm. "You haven't eaten like that in a while."

He nodded, though his hand still rested on his stomach. "Yeah, probably. I just need some rest."

"Let me get you some tea," I said, kissing his cheeks.

I made him some chamomile tea and sat beside him, watching the steam rise from the cup as I handed it to him. "It'll settle your stomach," I said softly, trying to sound more confident than I felt. He took a sip, then set the cup down beside him.

"Thanks, love," he murmured. "It's just… it doesn't feel like it's passing."

My chest tightened, but I nodded, trying to push the fear away. "Rest, Alasdair. I'm sure it's nothing. You've just had a long day."

But despite my words, a knot of worry began to grow in my stomach. Alasdair wasn't the type to complain, and seeing him so uncomfortable was unsettling. His usual strength seemed to have evaporated.

Hours passed, and it seemed the discomfort was only getting worse. I kept checking on him, but each time I did, his colour seemed a little off, his breathing a little more shallow. It wasn't just a bad stomach ache anymore.

"Love, maybe we should go to the hospital," I suggested.

He shook his head, his eyes closing briefly. "I don't know. I don't want to ruin our night, Sera. Let's just wait a little longer."

But I couldn't ignore it any longer. The signs were too clear. Something was wrong—something more than just a food-induced stomachache. I helped him sit up, supporting his weight as he slowly rose from the couch.

"You're not ruining anything."

Reluctantly, he agreed, and together, we made our way to the car. I tried to stay calm, focusing on the road as we drove through the darkened streets, my heart pounding with every passing second. I didn't know what was happening, but I knew that I couldn't lose him.

By the time we reached the hospital, he was clearly struggling. He was pale and sweating, and his discomfort had escalated to the point where he could hardly speak. The doctors took him in right away, their faces serious as they examined him.

"Seraphine," The doctor said, his voice calm but heavy with something unspoken. "We've received the results from Alasdair's post-surgery tests. We've been closely monitoring the area where the ulcer was removed, and I'm afraid there's something concerning we need to address."

My mind immediately jumped to the worst-case scenario, but I held on to hope. Maybe it's nothing.

"What is it?" I managed to ask.

The doctor paused for a moment before continuing. "Unfortunately, we've found that the area where the ulcer was treated has started developing cancerous cells."

My heart stopped.

I could feel everything around me dim as the words sunk in. Cancer? I hadn't prepared myself for this. I looked at Alasdair, his face pale against the hospital sheets, his eyes distant. He had been so strong, so determined, and now this unexpected, terrifying turn.

"Are you sure?" I asked, though the uncertainty in my voice betrayed my need for reassurance.

The doctor nodded. "Yes. We have seen evidence of malignancy in the tissue that was previously treated. It's still localised to the area, but it's a serious development. The cells are beginning to mutate."

I felt like I was losing control of my breath. The room suddenly felt too small. How could this be happening? The surgery had already been such a big step for him, and now, the word cancer was there, so real, so terrifying.

"The previous surgery was supposed to remove the affected tissue, but unfortunately, these new developments show that the cancer has taken root in that very area." The doctor's voice softened slightly, but the news didn't get any easier. "We will need to begin chemotherapy immediately to prevent the cancer from spreading further. It's going to be a tough journey, but we'll do everything we can to make sure the treatment works."

The idea of chemotherapy terrified me, but I knew it was our only chance. The road ahead would be long and uncertain, but I would be by his side every step of the way.

"I'll be here, Alasdair."

The tears I had been holding back fell freely now, but I didn't care. I would hold on to him. We would fight this all.

The years that followed felt like an endless cycle of hospital visits, treatments, and waiting. Chemotherapy had become a part of our lives, but it never seemed to work the way we had hoped. Each round of treatment left Alasdair weaker, his energy slowly drained, and his body fighting to keep up with the relentless toll the medication was taking. His hair had fallen out in patches, and the once-bright spark in his eyes began to fade, replaced by a tired resignation.

We had moments where things seemed almost normal—his laugh, though weaker, would echo through the apartment when we watched our favourite movies together. He would try to make jokes, despite the pain he was in, just to see me smile. But it was getting harder. The treatment was supposed to give us hope, but the cancer was stubborn, and we were losing the battle in slow motion.

"I don't know how much longer I can take this," he admitted one night, his voice hoarse as he leaned back on the couch.

I sat beside him, taking his hand, my own trembling slightly. "We'll keep going. One day at a time. You're strong."

But I could see the pain in his eyes, a depth of exhaustion that no amount of positive thinking could erase. Every time he went for a new round of treatment, there was a part of me that feared the worst. What if this was the one time the treatment would be too much for him? What if it broke him completely?

It was during one of his more difficult rounds of treatment that we received the news we had been dreading. The cancer had spread further, and the chemotherapy wasn't having the desired effect. The doctor was gentle with his words, but the truth still landed like a blow. "We'll try different combinations of medications, but at this point, it's becoming clear that this is going to be an uphill battle," he said.

I felt a sinking sensation in my chest, but I held it in. I couldn't show weakness, not now, not when he needed me most.

"We'll keep fighting," Alasdair said, his grip on my hand tightening. "We've come this far, haven't we?"

I nodded, blinking back tears. "We'll keep going. I'll be right here with you, through every step."

And so, we did. We fought, even when the odds seemed impossible. Even when it felt like the fight was slipping away from us, I couldn't give up. And neither could he. We held on to each other as tightly as we could, never letting go, even when the future was uncertain, even when the treatments weren't working the way we had hoped.

I didn't know what the future held. We had no guarantees. But I knew this much: I would love him through every moment, every struggle. No matter how difficult it got, no matter how painful, I would be right by his side—just as I promised.

## 38

# Seraphine

"Close your eyes," I called softly from outside his hospital room.

"Sera?" His voice was weak, yet curious.

"Yes, now close them!" I repeated, unable to keep the smile out of my voice.

"Alright, alright." I could hear the playful tone in his words as I pushed open the door and entered the room. I sat beside him, my heart racing with anticipation.

"You can open them now," I said.

He slowly opened his eyes, blinking in confusion. Then, his expression shifted, and he gasped.

"Oh, my Seraphine! What have you done to your hair?" His voice cracked slightly.

I had cut it shorter, just to my shoulders. It was a subtle change, but it was mine, a piece of me I wanted to share with him.

"I've got a surprise for you," I said, my smile widening as I reached behind my back and pulled out a small, carefully wrapped package.

I opened it to reveal the bright red wig. I placed it gently on his head, securing it with a tender touch.

"We're both redheads now," I said softly, my heart swelling with love for him.

He blinked at me, his hands reaching up to touch the wig, his face a mixture of disbelief and wonder. And then, as if everything he had been holding back finally broke free, his eyes filled with tears.

He pulled me into a hug, his arms wrapping around me with such intensity it almost knocked the breath out of me. He buried his face in my shoulder, his tears soaking into my shirt.

"I can't believe you'd do this for me," he cried.

I held him tighter, feeling the warmth of his embrace seep into me, grounding me in that moment. I wanted to tell him a lot of things but nature's call didn't let me.

"I'll be back. Gotta use the restroom." I said, breaking free from the hug. He nodded and let me go.

I spent longer in the restroom than usual, my stomach churning with what felt like an unsettling bout of diarrhoea. After what seemed like forever, I finally mustered the strength to leave. The hallway was quiet as I made my way back to the room, but when I reached the door, I noticed it was wide open.

As I stepped inside, I saw doctors and nurses gathered around him silently. I pushed through the crowd, my heart racing as I reached his bedside.

What I saw froze me.

Alasdair was lying motionless, his body covered in blood. It was pooling around him, staining the sheets as it slowly seeped from his mouth. His eyes were closed, his lips slightly parted in an eerie stillness that sent a chill through me.

"Doctor?" My voice trembled. "What's happening?"

The doctor turned to face me, his face pale and his eyes filled with sorrow.

"I'm so sorry."

"Sorry? Why are you sorry? He's fine." I said, taking his hand in mine. His forever-warm hands now felt colder than ice.

The doctor gently placed a hand on my shoulder, but I shrugged it off, desperate to be by his side.

"There's nothing more left to do, Seraphine." The doctor said softly.

"No, no, no, this isn't happening," I muttered to myself.

"I still have so much to say, so many promises to fulfil. This can't happen." I broke down, crying uncontrollably.

Everything joyful and lovely seemed to come to an end. My journey of being a poem came to an end.

# Epilogue

Feeling lost, feeling lonely, and feeling like I lost my only one, I started writing again. A book that contained my last words for him that I didn't get a chance to convey.

*My beloved poet,*

*Your words once wove the sky into verses, and the wind into whispers.*

*Now the silence hangs heavy, an unwritten poem that only I can feel.*

*Without you, every sentence falters, every page bleeds emptiness.*

*But I'll keep writing, for you live in every letter, in every line I dare to create.*

*Forever carrying your echoes,*

*Seraphine.*

I always wanted to be a poem and never a poet. So when I found my poet, I quit being one. But now that he's gone, I'm back to being what I always had been before I met him. And as the world moved on, I held his memory close, a love unspoken, yet eternal. A love that emerged between the lines.

**THE END**

Thank you for reading *Where Ink Hesitates!* If you enjoyed this book, I would be grateful if you could leave a review on the platform(s) of your choice.

Love,

Kankona

# About the author:

Kankona Chakraborty is a writer from India with a passion for weaving heartfelt stories of love and connection. Drawn to the intricacies of human emotions, Kankona brings romance to life through relatable characters and tender moments.

*Instagram: @konaspoetry*

www.ingramcontent.com/pod-product-compliance
Lightning Source LLC
LaVergne TN
LVHW041919070526
838199LV00051BA/2663